SWEET REVENGE

Lett Plunkett didn't have a night as fun as Fargo's. His cracked ribs from Fargo's bullet throbbed so bad he couldn't sleep, and he was cold in the night air. Having walked most of the day before, his feet ached almost as much as his wound.

He spent most of the night in a tree, hoping that some damned bear didn't climb up after him. Climbing the tree with his Sharps had been hard. Climbing down was even harder. With every move, Lett cussed the Trailsman and promised himself he'd get even with the son of a bitch sooner rather than later. All he had to do was get back to Denver City, which was a lot easier to think about than to do.

But Lett was going to get there even if it killed him. And when he did, he was going to gut Fargo with his bowie knife.

THE

TRAILSMAN

#283

COLORADO
CLAIM JUMPERS

by

Jon Sharpe

A SIGNET BOOK

SIGNET
Published by New American Library, a division of
Penguin Group (USA) Inc., 375 Hudson Street,
New York, New York 10014, USA
Penguin Group (Canada), 10 Alcorn Avenue, Toronto,
Ontario M4V 3B2, Canada (a division of Pearson Penguin Canada Inc.)
Penguin Books Ltd., 80 Strand, London WC2R 0RL, England
Penguin Ireland, 25 St. Stephen's Green, Dublin 2,
Ireland (a division of Penguin Books Ltd.)
Penguin Group (Australia), 250 Camberwell Road, Camberwell, Victoria 3124,
Australia (a division of Pearson Australia Group Pty. Ltd.)
Penguin Books India Pvt. Ltd., 11 Community Centre, Panchsheel Park,
New Delhi - 110 017, India
Penguin Group (NZ), cnr Airborne and Rosedale Roads, Albany,
Auckland 1310, New Zealand (a division of Pearson New Zealand Ltd.)
Penguin Books (South Africa) (Pty.) Ltd., 24 Sturdee Avenue,
Rosebank, Johannesburg 2196, South Africa

Penguin Books Ltd., Registered Offices:
80 Strand, London WC2R 0RL, England

First published by Signet, an imprint of New American Library,
a division of Penguin Group (USA) Inc.

First Printing, May 2005
10 9 8 7 6 5 4 3 2 1

The first chapter of this book previously appeared in *Kansas Weapon Wolves*,
the two hundred eighty-second volume in this series.

Copyright © Penguin Group (USA) Inc., 2005
All rights reserved

PUBLISHER'S NOTE
This is a work of fiction. Names, characters, places, and incidents either are the
product of the author's imagination or are used fictitiously, and any resemblance
to actual persons, living or dead, business establishments, events, or locales is
entirely coincidental.

The Trailsman

Beginnings . . . they bend the tree and they mark the man. Skye Fargo was born when he was eighteen. Terror was his midwife, vengeance his first cry. Killing spawned Skye Fargo, ruthless, cold-blooded murder. Out of the acrid smoke of gunpowder still hanging in the air, he rose, cried out a promise never forgotten.

The Trailsman they began to call him all across the West: searcher, scout, hunter, the man who could see where others only looked, his skills for hire but not his soul, the man who lived each day to the fullest, yet trailed each tomorrow. Skye Fargo, the Trailsman, the seeker who could take the wildness of a land and the wanting of a woman and make them his own.

*Denver City, 1858—there's gold in Cherry Creek
if you can hang on to your claim—
something that's not easy for a dead man to do.*

1

Afterward, the man with the lake-blue eyes couldn't have said exactly what it was that warned him.

It might have been some sound that he didn't even know he'd heard.

It might have been the absence of sound, the sudden end of birds calling and fluttering or of squirrels chattering.

It might even have been nothing more than instinct, honed and kept sharp by years on the trail when there was no one but himself to watch his back, front, and sides.

Whatever it was that warned him, Skye Fargo was out of the saddle and rolling to one side when he heard the bullet smack into the pine tree that was now in front of him. And by the time the sound of the shot had followed the bullet, his heavy Colt was already in his hand.

A second bullet thudded into the soft trunk of the pine sending bark chips flying, and Fargo's big Ovaro stallion, who was smarter than some humans Fargo had known, wandered off into the brush where he couldn't be easily seen.

Fargo was glad the horse was well hidden, but the trouble was that his attacker couldn't be easily seen, either. Fargo let his eyes roam over the intense green of the surrounding pines. There was no sign of a shooter, but there were plenty of places he could be hiding.

Fargo sighed. It was too nice a day to have to deal

with bushwhackers. The sun was shining up in the blue sky, and the smell of the pines was strong and sweet.

A bullet chipped off a limb above Fargo's head, and he looked across the trail to a wide place a good way up ahead, where a rocky outcropping jutted from a thin line of cedars. Fargo thought he saw a thin gray haze of gun smoke slowly rising above the cedars, but he could have been imagining it. So he lay there, listening to the unnatural quiet, and waited.

No more shots were fired, and after a few minutes the familiar sounds started to return. A couple of squirrels started up an argument over who had the right of way on a limb, a woodpecker began hammering at a tree trunk, and something moved heavily back in the brush. Not a man, Fargo thought. Most likely it was the Ovaro, though it might be a bear. It was late enough in the spring for bears to be out and roaming around, so Fargo took a look around. He caught a glimpse of the Ovaro, and turned back to look at the outcropping again.

There was no movement, and Fargo wondered who had taken a shot at him. He knew that whoever it was hadn't followed him from Kansas. He'd crossed too much open ground for anyone to follow him unnoticed, and even if he'd been in a thicket, he'd have known if anyone had been behind him. If Fargo knew anything at all, he knew about finding his way from one place to another, and about spotting anyone who might be tracking him.

Nobody had been. He was sure of that much, which meant that someone had been waiting for him. He wondered why, and he wondered how they'd known where he'd be. There were plenty of people who'd wanted him dead at one time or another, so many that Fargo had pretty much lost count, but he didn't think any of that bunch would know where he happened to be at this particular time.

He wondered how many shooters were hiding out there. Could be only one, he thought. An ambush didn't require any more than that. But he was pretty sure there were at least two. The second shot had come too soon for it to have been fired from the same rifle as the first, unless that shooter could reload a Sharps faster than just about anybody Fargo had ever known or heard of.

Fargo wondered if the bushwhackers were as patient as he was. He'd spent most of his life on the trail, in the woods, and under the open sky away from towns and people. He'd learned patience a long time ago.

It could be that whoever had taken the shots at him would think he'd been hit. If that was the case, sooner or later they'd have to come out and see if he was dead— either that or just ride off, thinking that maybe he wouldn't come after them.

He hoped they'd come to check on him. He could ask them all those things he was wondering about, and ask them none too gently, either.

Red Stover leaned back against the smooth rock and spit a stream of tobacco juice on the dirt. "Reckon I got him. Pounded his ass right out of that saddle with the first shot."

"Don't think so," Lett Plunkett said.

Red's beady eyes narrowed. "You sayin' you got him? You thinkin' you'll get more pay if you're the one killed him?"

Lett was tall and wide and looked mean as a grizzly, which he was. But this time he wasn't looking for an argument.

"Ain't saying nothin' of the kind, nor lookin' for any extra pay. I'm just sayin' that he's not hit."

"The hell he ain't." Red had the temper that was supposedly typical of all redheads, though his own hair had faded to a peculiar shade of orange. "You saw him fall soon's I shot him. I didn't miss."

Lett's voice remained mild. "Ain't sayin' you missed, and I ain't sayin' he didn't fall."

Red spit again and wiped his mouth with the back of his hand.

"You're one agreeable son of a bitch, ain't you?" he said.

"Ain't sayin' I agree with you."

"Then what in thunderin' hell *are* you sayin'?"

Lett didn't answer for a few seconds, and a dark flush started to creep up Red's neck and onto his face.

"You slow-talking bastard," Red said. "You tell me what you're thinkin', or by God I'll turn this Sharps on *you*."

"You wouldn't want to do that," Lett said, and Red knew he was right.

In the short time that Red had known Lett, he'd seen the big outlaw kill one man with his bare hands and rip another one from asshole to appetite with the big bowie knife he carried in a scabbard that hung from his belt. No matter how mad he got, Red wasn't going to try anything with Lett.

At least not while Lett could see him. If Lett turned his back, well, that was a whole different story. Red wasn't afraid of anybody who had his back turned.

"I'm just a little nervy, I guess," Red said by way of apology. "But I sure thought I shot that fella."

"He was too fast for us," Lett said. "He fell, all right, but he was already halfway out of the saddle before you pulled the trigger. I don't know what tipped him off, but somehow or other he knew we were here and gunnin' for him."

"No way he could've known," Red said.

"Maybe not. You know what they call him?"

"That fella we're supposed to kill? Yeah. Name's Fargo, but they call him the Trailsman. So what?"

"So he's not as easy to kill as some tenderfoot pecker-head. We should've been more careful."

"Don't think we could've been."

"Maybe not," Lett said. "The thing is, he's still alive, and he's out there waitin' for us to come for him."

"We could fool him," Red said, not liking that idea. "We could go get our horses and get out of here."

"Yeah, and not get paid. How would you like that?"

Red admitted that he wouldn't like it one bit. He wanted the money, as he'd already planned on spending some of it for whiskey and a whore.

"So what're we gonna do?" he asked.

"What the hell do you think?" Lett said. "We're gonna go get him."

Red wasn't so sure he wanted to do that, but he wasn't going to cross Lett. Better the devil you know, he thought, than the devil you don't.

"Where you reckon he is?" he asked.

"Behind that tree where we saw him fall. Unless he's moved, in which case he could be anywhere. What the hell difference does it make?"

It didn't make any difference, and Red knew it. As much as he wanted to get out of there and forget the whole thing, he wanted the money more. And he was more afraid of Lett than any damn Trailsman.

"You got a plan?" Red asked.

"Yeah," Lett said.

"Let's have it then."

So Lett told him what it was.

2

It was supposed to be an easy job.

Fargo had been in Leavenworth, having gone there when he got word of the gold strike at Cherry Creek out in the Colorado country. He could use a little cash money, and he figured he could find a party in Leavenworth that needed a guide without having to look too hard. As it happened, he found something even better.

Or something better found him. He'd been in Leavenworth less than a day when a well-dressed man in a new-looking bowler hat came up to him on the street and said, "Are you Skye Fargo?"

"Who wants to know?"

"Mr. Seth Rogers. Do you know who he is?"

Fargo said that he'd heard of Rogers.

The man nodded as if he'd expected that answer. "Just about everybody has. I'm John Stewart, and I work for him. He heard you were in town looking for work, and he wants to offer you a job."

"I just got here last night," Fargo said.

"Mr. Rogers has a lot of friends around town. One of them must have told him."

"What kind of a job is he offering?"

"That's for Mr. Rogers to tell you." Stewart handed Fargo a card with small printing. "That's Mr. Rogers's business address there on the card. He'll be in the office for the rest of the day if you'd like to talk to him. I think I can promise it'll be worth your while."

Fargo glanced down at the address, then looked back at the man in the bowler.

"I'll stop by there later in the day," he said.

"I'll let Mr. Rogers know," Stewart said. "Good day to you."

And with that and a nod, he turned and went on his way.

Fargo watched as he walked away, mingling with the other people on the street, and thought of what he knew about Seth Rogers. Rogers and his partner, Thomas Luman, had formed a freighting company in the early 1850s and made a pile of money hauling goods out west. Fargo couldn't rightly figure what kind of job a freighter would have for him, but he thought it might be worth looking into. After he'd eaten a meal of steak and potatoes, he located Rogers's office.

A young man wearing sleeve garters and a visor sat at a desk scratching on a piece of paper with a pen. He looked up when Fargo entered the room and asked if he could help.

"Mr. Rogers asked me to stop by," Fargo said. "Name's Fargo."

The man pushed back his chair and stood up. "Oh, yes. Mr. Stewart said you might be coming by. Mr. Rogers is looking forward to meeting you."

He opened the door to the office behind him and stepped inside.

"Mr. Fargo is here," he said, and a voice inside the room replied, "Send him on in."

The young man stepped aside, holding the door, and Fargo went past him into the room. Rogers, a stout, balding man with black eyes, sat behind a heavy oak desk. He wore a suit and vest. A gold watch chain draped across his ample stomach. Afternoon sunlight fell on the wooden floor through a window to Fargo's left.

Rogers stood and extended a hand across the desk.

"Seth Rogers," he said. "Pleased to meet you, Mr. Fargo."

Fargo took the hand and shook it. Rogers had a dry, firm grip, but he didn't try to crush Fargo's knuckles. There seemed to be no challenge in the man's hand.

"Have a seat, Mr. Fargo," he said.

"Thanks," Fargo said, and sat in a straight-backed wooden chair near the desk.

"I've heard a lot about you. People say you know this country like nobody else."

"Which country would you be talking about?"

Rogers, who had remained standing, waved an arm as if to indicate the whole continent. "This one. All of it."

"Don't know much about the East," Fargo said. "I stay pretty much on this side of the Mississippi."

"The West is the country I mean," Rogers said. He sat back down in his chair. "You know it from one end to the other."

Fargo couldn't think of anything to say to that, so he kept quiet.

"What I'm looking for," Rogers said when Fargo made no response, "is someone to do a little trail-blazing for me. I'll pay you well, but you'll have to work fast."

"What kind of a trail?" Fargo asked.

"I suppose you've heard of the Pikes Peak gold strike."

"I've heard enough to know it doesn't have anything to do with Pikes Peak."

Rogers laughed. "Well, you're right about that. The gold's north of there, where Cherry Creek comes into the South Platte River." He stood up and turned to the map behind him. Placing a finger on it, he said, "Right about here."

Fargo nodded.

Rogers dropped his arm to his side. "The thing is that people like the sound of 'the Pikes Peak strike.' Lots of folks have heard about that mountain, and they'd like to see it. Gives them another excuse to strike out for the goldfields."

"You were saying something about a trail," Fargo pointed out.

"Indeed. Thank you for reminding me. Sometimes I allow myself to drift off the track." Rogers ran his finger along a line on the map. "Here we have the Oregon Trail. I'm sure you're familiar with it." He lowered his arm and traced another line. "And this is the Santa Fe Trail, another one you know all about."

"I've traveled them," Fargo said.

"I was certain you had. As you can see, however, neither of them goes near Cherry Creek. The closest that either one comes, really, is the Santa Fe at Bent's Fort, and that's not very close."

Fargo said he could see that. He thought he knew now where Rogers might be heading with all this talk.

"What about the Smoky Hill Trail?" he asked.

"That's the way most people will be going if they leave from Kansas," Rogers said, "but it's not exactly what we're looking for."

Fargo thought Rogers was drifting again. "Maybe you'd better tell me exactly what it is you *are* looking for."

"My partner, Thomas Luman, and I are looking for our own trail."

"You planning to haul freight to Cherry Creek on a new trail?" Fargo asked.

Rogers turned away from the map and sat at his desk. "Not exactly, Mr. Fargo, though you're half right. Luman and I are going to begin a new enterprise. We're going to add a passenger service to our freight business. We plan to lay a road to Cherry Creek and organize a stage and express line to travel it. We believe we can make the trip in a stage in seven days, or even six."

"You're looking for a straight line, then," Fargo said. "Sort of split the difference between the two main trails and maybe sort of parallel the Smoky Hill Trail."

"That's the idea. As straight a line as we can make it, that's what we'd like to find. What do you think?"

What Fargo thought was that Rogers was going to be spending a lot of money on an enterprise that might peter out at any time, sooner rather than later if the gold didn't last. And it would be an expensive business to run, too. Stations to be built, horses and drivers to feed, horseshoes, smithing tools, guns, ammunition, wagons, stages. It all added up. And one couldn't really trust freight drivers—they'd steal and abandon cargo along the trail if they thought the load was too heavy.

"I hope you've thought this all the way through," Fargo said.

"Oh, you can count on that," Rogers told him. "The

route will be about seven hundred miles, meaning we'd need twenty-five to thirty stations. We've already got a price on fifty new Concord coaches, and we know a man who can supply us with eight hundred mules to pull them. Of course, hiring the drivers, men to tend the stock and keep the harness in good repair, will come later. And we'll need good men as our station agents."

He'd thought it out, all right. Fargo had to admit it. He'd even come up with a few things Fargo hadn't considered. Anyway, it was Rogers's problem, not his. Rogers had been in the freight business for a good while, and he should know what he was getting into with this new venture. Fargo didn't try to tell him anything. "You'd be sending me to look for a trail where you could build some way stations."

"Between twenty-five and thirty of them, as I said. One for every twenty-five miles of the trail. You'd also be helping us find some good locations."

Fargo thought it over. It seemed like a simple enough job, and it would be better than guiding a party of gold hunters out to Cherry Creek. He wouldn't have to deal with any cantankerous pilgrims who as often as not fell to quarreling and squabbling among themselves before the trip was half over.

"This is the kind of job you can do better than anyone," Rogers said to encourage him. "And I assure you that I'll pay you as much as any party you might guide out that way. What do you say?"

"You could just wait a few months. Before long those gold-crazy prospectors will have blazed you a trail that you could follow."

"They'll stick to the Smoky Hill Trail, for the most part, and even if they don't, Luman and I can't afford to wait. We want to get things started as soon as possible. We don't want someone else to beat us to setting up the kind of service we'll be offering. Someone else is bound to come up with the idea sooner or later, and we want to be well established before that happens."

"Might cost you a little more if I have to push it," Fargo said, trying to gauge just how eager Rogers really was.

Rogers didn't blink. "I'll pay you twice your usual fee if you'll start tomorrow."

Fargo allowed himself a thin smile. "You really are in a hurry, then. That's a lot of money. Is there anything I need to worry about out there?"

"Nothing but Indians. Cheyenne and Arapaho, and they don't seem to be causing much trouble these days. I just want to be sure this gets done without wasting any time."

Fargo unlimbered his lanky frame and stood up. "I'm your man, then. I'll get started in the morning."

Rogers rose and they shook hands again.

"You can get any supplies you need at Franklin's Mercantile. I'll send word that you're coming by, and you can charge everything to me."

"I travel light," Fargo said.

"But you'll need coffee, bacon, an extra canteen, all that sort of thing. Get whatever you need. I don't want you having to look around for provender while you're on the trail."

Fargo thought that Rogers was going to be a good man to work for.

"You don't have any other trails you need blazed, do you?" he said.

"Not at the moment, but if this venture is successful, there might be another job or two for you in the future. Assuming, of course, that this one turns out to be mutually satisfactory."

"I can't think of any reason why it wouldn't work out that way," Fargo said.

"Me neither," Rogers said. "Luman will be at a hotel when you arrive. There are a couple of towns there already, Denver City and Auraria. He's in Denver City, and you can report to him. I'll have an agreement drawn up this afternoon. Before you leave tomorrow, come by here and we can sign it."

"I'll be leaving mighty early."

"Don't worry about that. I'll be here."

"Then so will I," Fargo told him.

3

That was the way things had gone—a quick agreement, a handshake, a simple job to be done.

It had been simple, too, right up until the moment that somebody had tried to shoot Fargo out of the saddle. He had only a day's worth of traveling left, and the trail would have been ready for the surveyors. Now it looked as if there might be a slight delay.

He knew he wasn't going anywhere. Whoever wanted him dead was going to have to come after him. They couldn't really afford just to ride off and leave him there. They'd have to be sure their job was finished before they hightailed it.

Fargo moved to a comfortable place of concealment where the limbs of a pine swept the ground. Here he'd be able to see anyone who was coming before they saw him.

Fargo waited. It didn't pay to rush things when there was shooting involved. About three-quarters of an hour passed when he heard rustling from the brush.

They were pretty good, he thought, not making any more noise than a couple of rutting moose. One was creeping along from his left, the other from the right, obviously planning to catch him in the middle. They might even have had a chance if he'd still been behind the tree where he'd been at first.

The man on the right was about as big a fella as Fargo had ever seen. He was as big as a grizzly and wore a bowie knife on his belt. His Sharps rifle glinted in a patch of sunlight.

The other man had stringy, orange hair that hung out from under his hat. He also had a Sharps and looked a little fidgety as he made his way through the trees.

"That was his horse I saw back there," he said. "Bound to have been. Ain't nobody else around here. Where the hell's he gotten off to?"

Fargo stepped out from behind the limbs, holding the Colt where the men could see it.

"I'm right here," he said. "Why don't you two put those rifles down on the ground, and we'll have a talk about why you tried to kill me."

The man on Fargo's left twitched nervously, but the big one on the right didn't appear in the least perturbed. He said, "Maybe it's you who better lay down your gun, friend. You might be able to get one of us, but not both of us. The last one standin' would be me or Red."

"You tell him, Lett," Red said, with only a slight quaver in his voice. "We got the advantage, just like you said we would."

That might have been the case if Fargo had intended to waste any more time talking, but he didn't even consider that possibility. He shot the big man in the chest, and a red stain appeared on his dirty shirt. Before Lett had even hit the ground, Fargo turned his still-smoking pistol toward Red.

"Jesus, you killed Lett!" Red said.

Lett hit the ground, and brown pine needles popped up around him. The rifle dropped from his hands. He lay there, his right foot twitching rapidly. After a couple of seconds it stopped, and Lett didn't move.

"I'll kill you, too," Fargo said to Red, "if you don't put that rifle down. I'd rather talk to you than shoot you, but you have to help me out."

"You killed Lett," Red repeated. He couldn't seem to believe what had just happened. "He said we'd have the advantage."

"He's no big loss," Fargo said. "You didn't have the advantage, so he wasn't near as smart as you thought he was. Now why don't you put down that rifle and we'll have us a palaver."

Red started to do as Fargo had suggested, but just before the rifle touched the ground, he jerked it up and pointed it in Fargo's direction.

If the Trailsman had more time to think about things, he would have shot Red in the arm or leg, but as it was, his instincts took over. The big Colt roared, and a red spot bloomed in the middle of Red's forehead. His hat flew off, and the man crumpled to his knees. For a couple of seconds, his uncomprehending eyes stared straight ahead. His face jerked up as if he might be looking for something in the treetops. There was nothing there. His face turned down, and he fell forward into the dead pine needles. The back of his head was gone.

"Damn," Fargo said.

He'd hoped to find out why the two men had wanted him dead, and now they were both dead instead. And he was stuck with the bodies. He sure as hell wasn't going to bury them, as he doubted they'd have done it for him, but it was a long day's ride to Cherry Creek. If he tried to haul them in on their horses, they'd start to get ripe. Still, he hated to leave them lying where they lay.

He holstered his Colt and looked at the two men, wishing things had turned out a little differently. No use worrying about it now, though, so he went to look for their horses.

The horses were just about where Fargo had thought they'd be, not too far from the rock outcropping where Red and Lett had concealed themselves. Fargo led the horses back to where the two men were lying, wondering how he was going to get Lett up across the saddle. Red wouldn't be any trouble, but Lett was a different story. He was a load. It would be like trying to hoist a dead grizzly bear. Fargo wasn't sure he was up to the job.

As it turned out, he didn't have to worry about it. When he got back, Red was still lying there flat on his face, but Lett was gone.

A man who'd called himself Doctor Nathaniel Donaldson had once told Lett that he was different from ordinary men. Lett didn't know if the man was a real doctor or not. He worked the mining towns with a medicine wagon, selling Donaldson's Miracle Cure, guaranteed to cure everything from the night trembles to mange. Lett figured it might do the job on the mange, but he wasn't so sure about anything else.

"It's not just that you're big as an ox," Donaldson said. "Anybody can see that with one eye closed. You're different in another way, one I ain't sure I've ever seen before."

Lett knew he was different. Women liked him and men feared him. There weren't all that many men who could say the same.

"It ain't that, either," Donaldson said.

Donaldson had been drinking some of his Miracle Cure, and he offered the bottle to Lett, who was working for him as a kind of bodyguard, making sure that none of the rubes sneaked up to the wagon during the night and tried to get their money back.

Lett motioned the bottle away. He'd put the stuff on a sick dog, but he wasn't about to put any of it in his stomach. What he wanted to know was what the doc was talking about.

"You just don't give a damn, is what," Donaldson said. "Most men, even the best and the worst of 'em, care about something or other. Money. Liquor. Women. Something. But not you. You just don't give a damn."

"I like all those things you said," Lett told him. "Nothing wrong with money and whiskey. I wouldn't mind having a drink right now."

Donaldson held out the Miracle Cure, but Lett shoved his hand away.

"Not that stuff. The real thing."

"This is close enough for me," Donaldson said, and took another swallow. He looked at Lett through bleary eyes. "You don't even care if you live or die."

Lett thought over what the doc had said and decided that the old man knew what he was talking about. It wasn't that Lett didn't like the things the doc had mentioned, but he could do without them. He didn't care one way or the other. As for living and dying, he'd never even thought about it. You were either alive or you were dead, and if you were dead, you wouldn't know it. So why worry? Everyone else did, but not Lett. And, now that the doc had mentioned it, that did indeed make him different.

From that time forward, Lett had known that while he walked among other men, he wasn't like them. He was different, better, a man set apart.

Lying there now, Lett knew that the ball from Fargo's pistol would have killed an ordinary man, exploded his heart like a rotten melon—but it hadn't killed Lett. It had knocked him flat, knocked the breath right out of him, but it hadn't killed him. And it wasn't too surprising to Lett that he didn't much care, one way or the other.

While Fargo was gone looking for the horses, Lett sat up and looked around him. He felt like he'd been kicked in the chest by a government mule. He also hurt like hell, and his shirt was bloody, but he thought he could get up and walk away if he wanted to. Which he did. He didn't see any profit in waiting around until Fargo came back.

He stood slowly, then picked up his rifle. Just bending over sent pain shooting through him. Every breath he took burned, and something grated in his chest, but Lett didn't let any of it bother him too much. He didn't allow himself to care.

After he had the rifle firmly in hand and had determined that he wasn't going to fall back down, Lett looked over to where Red lay. He didn't care about Red, either, the dumb son of a bitch. Instead of talking, he should have just shot the Trailsman and ended the fuss.

He walked over to the body and gave it a nudge with his toe, just to make sure that Red wasn't alive. Red didn't move, and Lett nudged him again, a little harder. He would have kicked the hell out of Red, but that might have started his chest to hurting. So he didn't bother. Red wasn't worth the trouble. Besides, from the way the back of his head looked, there really wasn't any chance of him moving, no matter how hard anybody kicked him.

Lett thought Fargo would be back at any time, so he forgot about Red and walked away into the trees, holding his hand pressed hard against his chest. That seemed to help a little.

What Lett didn't know was that Fargo's pistol ball had hit one of his ribs. The rib had broken, but the ball had been deflected to the left, digging a trench along the rib under Lett's flesh before tearing through at his side. It was a painful wound, and aggravating, but far from a mortal one.

What Lett did know was that for once in his life, he cared about something. It was a strange feeling, but he knew it was real. He cared about Fargo because the son of a bitch had hurt him. No one had ever really hurt Lett before, and he was going to do something about it. He was going to get Fargo, sooner or later, and make him hurt. Lett had been given the job of killing him, and he'd messed it up. That didn't bother him, but the fact that Fargo had hurt him was different.

Sooner or later there'd be another chance at Fargo, Lett thought, and he'd make the most of it. Maybe it would come even sooner than he hoped.

He pushed aside a pine branch and walked slowly on, breathing shallowly, his hand pressed to his chest.

"I'll be damned," Fargo said when he got back with the horses and saw that Lett was gone.

Fargo knew he was a good shot, and he knew he'd hit Lett in what appeared to be a vital spot, but it was always a mistake to leave anything to chance. Fargo had learned that lesson a long time ago. He should have checked to make sure Lett was dead, but he had taken his skill with a pistol for granted, and now Lett was off in the brush with his Sharps.

It didn't take Fargo long to find out which way Lett had gone, as the bushwhacker hadn't made any effort to conceal his path, but the Trailsman didn't go after him. He wasn't going to give Lett another shot at him. Lett wasn't much good with a rifle, judging by his earlier effort, but anybody could get lucky, hiding off in the trees and shooting from cover. And the very fact that Lett was alive proved that he was luckier than he had any right to be.

So Fargo heaved Red across the saddle of one of the spare horses, whistled up the Ovaro, and moved on.

4

Fargo had been in mining towns before, so he knew what to expect: wooden frame buildings hurriedly thrown together, tents, and even two or three more substantial structures, and people milling around on the boardwalk and in the rutted main street that would be a quagmire if it ever rained. Even though it was nearly midnight, most of the men Fargo saw were drunk or well on the way, some of them hooting and hollering. There were lights in the saloons, though hardly anywhere else. The few respectable folks in town had long ago closed their stores and gotten away from the noise and carousing.

Fargo rode the Ovaro past a couple of the saloons, which were built better and looked more permanent that most of the other buildings, looking for something that might be a sheriff's office or jail. He drew a couple of curious glances, but hardly anybody paid him any mind. It probably wasn't the first time they'd seen someone coming into town with a dead body slung across a horse's back. Mining towns had more killings than ordinary places, but no matter how raw the place was, sooner or later there was an attempt at setting up some kind of law. Fargo wondered if the people in Denver City had gotten around to that yet.

Because he didn't want to haul the dead body around any longer than he had to, Fargo had decided to ride on into town instead of camping for the night, even if it meant pushing things a bit faster than he'd planned. It hadn't been quite as far to the town as he thought, but it had still taken him the rest of the day and most of the evening to get there. He needed to find a livery stable for the Ovaro and the other two horses, get them rubbed down and fed, but he wanted to get rid of Red first.

He hadn't gone too far past the saloons before he came to a makeshift jail. It didn't look nearly as solid as the saloons, but it would do to hold somebody like Red, who wasn't likely to break out.

Fargo stopped in front of the building and tied the horses to the hitching rail in front. Scrawled on the door in black paint was the word SHERIFF. There was a light on inside, so Fargo went in.

The light came from a flickering coal oil lamp sitting on a battered desk. There was a man behind the desk, but he wasn't doing any paperwork. He was tilted back in the chair, his feet up on the desk, his hat over his eyes to keep out the light. He wasn't snoring, but his breathing indicated to Fargo that he was asleep.

Not that it mattered, as there were no prisoners in either of the two cells. Fargo had never known of a mining town that didn't have at least one or two residents in jail, given the general rowdiness of the inhabitants, but maybe Denver City was an exception.

A shotgun leaned against the wall within easy reach, and a couple of rifles were chained in a rack on the wall. If there was any trouble, the sheriff would be ready for it, but the empty cells seemed to indicate that there wasn't much trouble in Denver City. Fargo noticed that there were no wanted posters on the walls, though there was a stack of them on the sheriff's desk. Fargo could see only the top one, as they were in a stack that didn't look as if it had been disturbed recently, if ever.

Fargo stood by the open door and rapped on it with his knuckles. The man at the desk twitched a little but didn't wake up, so Fargo rapped again.

The man snorted and pushed up his hat with his right thumb. He blinked a couple of times as the light hit his eyes and said, "Yeah, what do you want?"

He was skinny, his eyes were too close together, and

he needed a shave. Fargo couldn't hold that against him, as he could have used a shave himself. But Fargo planned to take care of that little detail as soon as he could, whereas the sheriff looked as if he didn't much care if he shaved again or not.

"I have a dead man outside," Fargo said.

The sheriff leaned forward on the desk, looking up at Fargo. "If he's dead, why in the hell did you bring him here?"

"Aren't you the sheriff?" Fargo said.

The man opened a drawer in the desk and rummaged around in it for a couple of seconds. Then he grunted in satisfaction and brought out a dull silver badge that he pinned to his shirt.

"You're damned right I'm the sheriff. Name's Tank. Tank Olson. Now let me ask you again. Why did you bring a dead man to me?"

"Because I thought that the law ought to be notified. Wouldn't it be your job to find out why he was dead?"

"Hell, I don't give a damn if he's dead or alive." Olson noticed Fargo's skeptical look and added, "But you can tell me about it if you want to."

"He and a friend set up an ambush and tried to kill me," Fargo said. "But they didn't. I killed one of them instead."

Olson stood up. Slowly.

"All right, then. I like a man who can tell it and get it over with. Let's have a look at him."

Fargo went back outside, and Olson followed. When they reached the horses, Olson walked around to the side of the one carrying Red. He grabbed hold of Red's chin and lifted the head to catch a little of the light that came out of the jail door.

"Red Stover," Olson said. "He's been in trouble around here a time or two. I figured he might end up like this, sooner or later."

"I'd like to know why he took a shot at me," Fargo said. "I thought you might have some ideas."

"I don't believe I caught your name," Olson said.

"Skye Fargo."

Olson looked him over. "You the fella they call the Trailsman?"

"That's me."

Olson nodded. "Yeah, I've heard of you. But as to any ideas about why Red might take a shot at you, I don't have one. Maybe he just didn't like your looks."

"He didn't get close enough to look at me," Fargo said.

"Well, you never know with a fella like Red. He had a temper. Liable to shoot at a fella as not. You better take him down to Sloane's."

"Sloane's?"

"Barbershop. Down that way." Olson pointed. "He does some undertaking, too. He'll see to it that Red gets planted proper."

"And that's it? No investigation? No questions?"

Olson spit into the dry dirt of the street. "Look here, Fargo. I'm the sheriff, but all I do is try to keep down the property damage and killing here in town. If anybody gets killed out on the trail, well, I figure that's just his hard luck. None of my business. So you just take old Red down to Sloane's and forget about him. That's what I plan to do."

It seemed to Fargo like a funny way to run a sheriff's office, but he wasn't going to complain. He'd thought that getting rid of Red's body would require a lot of explaining, and he was glad to find out that he'd been wrong. He did have one thing to add, however.

"There was someone with him. Big man. Built like a bear."

Olson didn't even have to think about it. "That would be Lett Plunkett. He and Red have been runnin' buddies for a while."

"Lett ever get into any trouble?"

"None that he couldn't get out of without my help. I don't get paid enough to go up against somebody like him, and if anybody else wants to try him out, they've bought their own trouble. You didn't kill Lett, did you?"

Fargo thought there was a somewhat hopeful note in

Olson's voice. If there was, he was going to be disappointed.

"No," Fargo said. "I didn't kill him. But I think I hurt him pretty bad."

"Goddamn. You might be sorry about that if he takes a notion to do something about it. How'd he get away from you? If he was hurt so bad, I mean."

Fargo told Olson what had happened.

"He's probably laid up somewhere, nursin' his wound like an old catamount," Olson said. He spit on the dirt again. "If you're lucky, he'll die."

Fargo thought that he never seemed to get lucky that way. He said, "And you don't have any idea why he might want to kill me, do you?"

"Not a single damned one. He was like Red. If there was trouble, he'd be in the middle of it. Either one of 'em would shoot you just for meanness."

Fargo figured he'd gotten about as much from the sheriff as he was going to get. And it wasn't much.

"What about a livery?" he said.

Olson had already started back into the jail. Probably wanted to sit back down and get his feet up, Fargo thought. The sheriff didn't even bother to turn around to answer.

"Keep on going past Sloane's. You'll come to it."

Fargo thanked him, but he wasn't sure that Olson heard. The sheriff had already closed the jail door.

Fargo had to bang on the barbershop door for a long time before anyone came. There was a pole out front, painted red and white, and a sign on the door read, SLOANE'S UNDERTAKING PARLORS in black crooked letters.

Fargo's knocking was finally answered by an old man wearing a dirty nightshirt and a cap. Fargo assumed it was Sloane himself.

"What the hell is it?" Sloane asked.

"Got a customer for you," Fargo said.

"I don't do no barberin' at this time of night. Come back in the mornin'."

He started to close the door, but Fargo put out a hand and stopped it.

23

"Damn it to hell," Sloane said. He snatched off his cap and rubbed his thin, stubbly hair. "Who do you think you are?"

"Name's Fargo. And like I said, I have a customer for you."

"And like I said, you damned well can come back in the mornin'."

"This fella won't wait," Fargo said.

Sloane tried to peer over Fargo's shoulder to see who might be waiting there with him.

"Impatient, is he? Well, that don't matter to me. He can shave his own face and cut his own hair, or he can wait. I'm goin' back to bed."

Sloane put his cap on and pulled it down with both hands. He tried to close the door, but Fargo stuck out his boot.

"This fella's not impatient, and he can wait forever if you want him to, but he'll be mighty ripe by then."

"Oh, hell." Sloane pulled the cap off again. His hair, what there was of it, stood up in little tufts. "So he's that kind of a customer. Why in the hell didn't you just say so?"

"You never gave me the chance."

"Don't mess around with me, young fella. You damned well did have time. You were just having some fun with an old man, and you might as well admit it."

Fargo had been shot at in the morning and on the trail all day. He didn't feel like arguing with the old undertaker any longer.

"All I want is to get rid of this body and find me a place to spend the night," Fargo said. "If you don't want to fool with him, that's fine with me. But I'm dumping him right here in front of your shop if you don't."

"Damn it." Sloane glared at Fargo. "You can't do that."

Fargo could, and he would. He said so.

"You probably would, you son of a bitch. All right, bring him around back, and I'll lay him out in the back room. You payin'?"

"No. Sheriff says this one's on the town."

"Sheriff says?" Sloane laughed. "That's a good one, Fargo. You gonna help me collect?"

"Not my job," Fargo said.

"Damned right it's not. You just bring in the body and dump him on me. I'm the one has to do all the work."

Fargo shrugged. "You want him here? Or in the back?"

"The back, damn it," Sloane said. "Take him on around. I'll meet you there."

Fargo led the horse carrying Red through the alley and around to the back of the barbershop/undertaking parlor. Sloane was waiting at the door and helped Fargo drag the body inside.

"He ain't stiff," Sloane said.

"He was for a while, but it passed off," Fargo said.

"Well, let's get him on the table there. He can wait till mornin', and then I'll see that he gets a good send-off. You want to attend the funeral?"

"Nope. Don't care to. Don't care how good the send-off is, either."

"Not exactly the best of friends, I take it."

"You could say that."

"I just did," Sloane told him, and made a cackling noise that Fargo assumed was a laugh.

Fargo didn't laugh. He wasn't in the mood for undertaker humor.

5

The livery stable was nothing but a big, unfinished barn, smelling of horse manure, oats, and hay. Its wide doors were open, but no one was exactly looking for business to come walking in at that time of night; however, the owner slept on the premises and was more alert than Sloane had been. He wasn't wearing a nightshirt, either, being fully dressed in faded denims that were out at the knees and a hat that looked like a horse might have chewed on it at some time or another. He yawned and stretched and told Fargo what the charges would be for taking care of the three horses.

"I'm not interested in paying for two of them," Fargo said. "What I want to do is sell them to you."

The liveryman, whose name was Carver, gave Fargo a suspicious look, knocked some straw off his shirt, and said, "You own 'em?"

"I do," Fargo said, which was more or less the truth.

"You got a bill of sale for 'em?"

"No. But I can promise you that nobody's going to come around and make any claim on them."

Carver looked skeptical. "You can, can you? And just how can you do that?"

"Well, the owner of one of them's down at Sloane's right now, getting laid out for burial. You might say I inherited the horse from him."

Carver stroked his beard. "So that's the way of it, eh? What about the owner of the other one? He down at Sloane's gettin' laid out, too?"

"That one's owner's disappeared. He forgot to tell me where he was going, so the way I look at it, he made me a gift of the horse. Like I told you, you don't have to worry about him coming by and making a claim on it."

Carver considered it for a few seconds. "I don't have to tell you that they're good horses. You can probably see that. I can't give you what they're worth."

Fargo wasn't interested in making a profit.

"Tell you what," he said. "Why don't you just take care of my Ovaro for me while I'm in town. When I leave, you can count the charges against the price of the horses. I'm sure we can come to an arrangement we'll both be satisfied with."

"What about the saddle tack? That ain't as good as the horses."

"I'm selling the saddles, too," Fargo said. "I'll make you a good deal."

Carver considered it. "You come here to try the prospectin'? How long you gonna be around?"

"I'm no prospector," Fargo said, "and I don't know how long I'll be staying." He hoped it wouldn't be long, but there was no need to tell Carver that. "Do you want the deal or not?"

"I'll take it. What did you say your name was?"

Fargo didn't think he'd said. "Fargo."

"All right, then, Mr. Fargo." Carver put out his hand. "We'll shake on it, and it's done."

Fargo took the hand, which was rough and calloused. Carver had a firm grip.

"You ever do any prospecting yourself?" Fargo asked.

"Nope. I figger the best way to make money in a place like this is get it off the ones that find it. So I set me up a little business and take whatever comes my way. I do all right."

Fargo was sure that was true. He turned the horses over to Carver and asked if there was a bathhouse in town.

"Sure enough. Right next to the Lucky Lady Saloon. You gonna get prettied up and have a go at some of the women?"

"I just want to bathe somewhere besides a cold creek for a change," Fargo said, handing over the reins to the Ovaro. "You take good care of my horse."

Carver took the reins. "You can count on that. Nobody takes better care of horses than I do. You can ask anybody in town about that."

Fargo removed his saddlebags and threw them over his shoulder.

"I'll see you later," he said, and walked back down the street.

The bathhouse was open. Fargo had expected it would be. Plenty of miners didn't come into town until well after dark, and the ones who'd had a little luck that day would want to get themselves "prettied up and have a go at the women," as Carver had put it. That was another thing Fargo knew about mining towns. The men who made money panning gold were likely to spend it as quickly as they got it, and they liked nothing better than to spend it on women and whiskey. Fargo knew that the owners of the Lucky Lady and the other saloons would leave Denver City a good bit richer than any of the miners.

Fargo went to the bathhouse and was met at the door by a short, bowlegged man who looked as if he might be seventy years old. He wore a battered black hat, patched denim pants, and a flannel shirt that was so faded Fargo couldn't guess what the original color might have been. His scraggly beard was gray, and so was the hair that stuck out from under the hat.

"Want a bath?" the man asked.

"How much?"

"Twenty-five cents for cold water, dime more if you want it hot. Or if you're near broke, you can use somebody else's water for ten cents."

Fargo wasn't interested in anybody's dirty water, and he didn't want the water to be cold, either. It was spring, but the nights were still plenty cool. Fargo said he wanted hot water.

"Then that's what you'll get. My name's Henry, and I'll fetch the fresh water. You can come on in."

Fargo followed Henry into the building. The slated floor was damp and slippery. Two long metal tubs sat in the first room. They were shaped like coffins, wide at the top and narrow at the bottom. Henry put out his hand. Fargo paid him, and the man went on through another door.

Fargo looked over the two unoccupied tubs. There was cold dirty water in one of them, but Fargo didn't intend to use that one. He hung his hat on a peg, put his saddle-bags over the back of a chair, and took off his boots.

Henry came in before Fargo was finished undressing. He had a bucket of heated water that he said he'd gotten from a boiler in a back room.

"Hop on in the tub," Henry said, "and I'll pour in the water."

Fargo removed the rest of his clothes and put them on the chair with his saddlebags. He hung his gun belt over the back of the chair and put it where he could reach it. Only then did he step over the side of the tub.

"Bet the ladies like you quite a bit," Henry said, giving him a look. "If you don't mind my sayin' so."

Fargo sat down in the tub and didn't respond. Henry poured in the water, and Fargo leaned back to enjoy the warmth.

"I'll go get another bucket," Henry said, and dis-appeared.

When he returned after what seemed too long a time to Fargo, he poured in another bucketful and went to fetch more. The deeper the water got, the more relaxed Fargo became. He could feel the tiredness draining out of him. After the water cooled a bit, he ducked his head under and soaked his hair. He came up blubbering and squeezed most of the water out.

Henry was through with his water hauling and seemed interested in conversation.

"Ain't seen you around here before," he said.

"I'm new in town," Fargo said. He didn't want to discuss his reason for being there. "Any charge for some soap?"

"Soap's free, long as you don't use all of it."

Henry retrieved a bar of soap from a shelf and handed it to Fargo, then left the room again. Fargo sat and held the soap, waiting for the last of the heat to leave the water.

Henry returned after a while. "You a prospector?"

"I'm just passing through," Fargo said, and lathered up.

The soap was grainy and had the smell of lye and ashes. Fargo hoped it didn't take off his skin along with the trail dirt.

"You might want to spend a little time next door in the Lucky Lady," Henry told him. "They got faro, three-card monte, and other interestin' games of chance. Girls, too. Miz Rose Malone's the owner, and she owns this bathhouse. She won't let any miners hop in the sack with her girls unless they're cleaned up."

Fargo rinsed away as much of the soap as he could and said it was nice to know that he wasn't the only one in town who cared about cleanliness.

"It ain't about folks bein' clean so much as that Miz Malone makes a profit off the baths, too. It all adds up, is the way she puts it."

It sounded to Fargo as if Rose Malone was an enterprising woman. He felt of his chin and said, "Is there a razor around here?"

"Sure is. Cost you five cents to use it, though."

Fargo had a razor in his saddlebags, but he didn't want to get it out, and he didn't want Henry to be looking in the bags.

"That's fine," he said. "What about a mirror? Any charge for that?"

"Mirror's free," Henry said, and went away.

He came back with a straight razor and a mirror, which he handed to Fargo. The mirror was cracked, but Fargo could see his reflection well enough. He lathered his face and scraped off the whiskers as well as he could. The razor could have used a stropping, but he figured Henry would charge him extra for that.

Fargo nodded, rinsed his face, and said, "Towel?"

Henry went away and came back with a thin towel. Fargo stood up and took it from him and started to dry off. While Fargo was drying his hair, he heard Henry say, "This is him, Miz Malone. Said his name was Fargo."

Fargo lowered the towel and tossed his hair out of his eyes. There in the room with him and Henry was a tall redheaded woman dressed in her saloon finery, appraising Fargo with a pair of pale green eyes.

Fargo was a little surprised to see her there, but he realized that Henry must have gone for her on one of his trips out of the room. It had been a long time since having a woman see him naked had embarrassed Fargo. Still, he was modest enough to wrap the towel around his waist.

"I told you he was a big 'un," Henry said.

The woman smiled. "And you were right."

Her voice was low and husky, and Fargo liked the way it sounded. She continued to study Fargo as if he were a prize bull. So while she looked him over, he did the same for her.

Her dress was cut low, and he saw the white mounds of her breasts. Her lips were red, though not the same color as her hair, and her wide mouth had the hint of a smile. Her hips were ample, and her buttocks looked round and firm. Fargo found himself wondering how she'd look if she took off the dress and if red was the natural color of her hair.

"Henry tells me you're new in town," she said.

Fargo looked at Henry, who looked at the floor as if he might be studying a unique water spot.

"I'm Rose Malone," the redhead said. "Don't blame Henry. He's been told to let me know whenever anybody interesting comes in for a bath. This is the first time he's done it."

"So Henry thought I might be interesting?" Fargo said.

Rose looked at the towel. "Yes. I'd say he was right, too, based on appearances alone."

"I've heard that appearances can fool you."

"We might have a chance to find out about that. That is, if you have no objections."

Fargo didn't object to getting to know a woman, especially attractive one like Rose Malone. But he wasn't exactly sure what she wanted from him.

"The thing is," she said, "I don't work the upstairs at my saloon. I don't think it's a good idea for the owner to be having carnal relations with her customers, and the other girls might object if they thought it was taking money out of their pockets."

"I can see that," Fargo said. "Makes good business sense."

"That's true. But sometimes a woman gets a little . . . lonely. She needs a man to keep her company for a while."

"Lots of men around here," Fargo said. "Plenty of them, I'd say."

"There are men, and there are men. The ones around here are mostly shiftless and uneducated. They don't have much in the way of conversation, and they don't know how to treat a lady. Do you?"

Fargo gave her a grin. "I've never had any complaints."

"I'll just bet you haven't."

"But I'm not much on education. I've read a book or two, but I've never been to any fancy schools."

"There's more to education than schooling," Rose said. "If you take my meaning."

"I think I do. Why don't you let me get dressed, and maybe we could have a drink. And a conversation."

"I've seen men get dressed before."

"So have I," Henry said, "but it don't give me no pleasure. I think I'll just step outside for a while if nobody minds."

He looked from Fargo to Rose and back at Fargo. Fargo gave him a nod. Henry grinned and started out the front door.

He didn't quite make it outside. Just as he reached the

opening, he was bowled over by the two men who came rushing in with guns in hand.

Even though there was no warning, Fargo's instincts took over just as they had on the trail. As soon as the two men burst into the room, Fargo pushed Rose Malone down, grabbed his gun belt, and dived behind the tub he'd bathed in.

Just about the time he hit the floor, the shooting started.

6

Two bullets twanged into the tub behind which Fargo had taken cover. Water spurted out and ran across the floor.

Fargo was about to rise up and fire a shot of his own when he discovered that the towel had fallen from around his waist.

"The hell with it," he said, and looked over the rim of the tub.

Two pistols cracked, and two bullets flew past Fargo's head, one of them so close that he was sure he heard it buzzing by.

Fargo had been shot at too often to let a bullet bother him. Instead of ducking back down, he shot one man in the center of the chest.

The man pulled back the hammer of his pistol, but by then his brain got the message that he was dead, and he fell backward, hitting the floor with a solid thud.

As he was falling, the second man ducked behind the chair where Fargo's clothes and saddlebags hung. Fargo didn't want to ruin his outfit by filling it with bullet holes, so he hesitated to shoot. Maybe the man would give up peacefully.

He heard a shrill whistle from his right. He looked over at Rose Malone, who sat in the floor with the thumb and first finger of her left hand at the corners of her mouth. She whistled sharply again, and this time the man behind the chair looked at her.

She shot him right in the middle of the forehead with the derringer she clutched in her right hand.

He sprawled face down across the floor. A small trickle of blood ran down his nose and onto the floor. The man Fargo had shot lay on his back nearby. He hadn't bled much either, but water was running all over the floor.

The room was full of acrid gun smoke, and Fargo's ears rang from the shooting. But he could hear Henry, who was lying on the floor like the two dead men. He had his hands clamped down on his hat, and he kept repeating, "Goddamn. Goddamn."

Fargo looked around for the towel. It was lying by him on the floor, and he rose to his knees and pulled it around him. Rose Malone was already on her feet, but Henry hadn't moved. He hadn't stopped saying "Goddamn," either.

Rose walked over to him. The derringer she had been holding had disappeared. She stuck a toe in Henry's ribs. "Get up, Henry. It's all over, and you're not shot."

Henry moved his hands off his head and looked up at her. "You right sure about that? I feel like I got blood all over me."

"That's water from the tub," Rose told him. She looked at the two dead men. "Those two are shot. You don't look like them, do you?"

Henry turned his head to the side and looked at the man Fargo had killed. Water dripped off the ends of the gray hairs of his beard.

"Goddamn," he said.

"I don't approve of cussing, Henry," Rose said. "You know that."

A whorehouse madam who didn't approve of cussing? Now Fargo had heard everything.

Fargo got into his pants as Rose helped Henry over to the chair and got him seated. Henry's wet clothing clung to his body.

"I'm not scared," Henry said. "I'm just too goddamned old to be gettin' shot at."

"Nobody was shooting at you," Rose said. "It looked like they were shooting at Mr. Fargo."

"Might as well have been shootin' at me. Bullets flyin' ever'where. A man could get killed. Haulin' water, that's fine. Fetch this, carry that. I can do that. But no shootin'. I didn't hire on for shootin' and havin' people tryin' to kill me."

"I think they were more interested in killing Mr. Fargo than in killing you," Rose said. "Why do you think that is, Mr. Fargo?"

Fargo pulled on his buckskin shirt. "All I know is that it's the second time it's been tried lately."

He told them about Red and Lett and what had happened on the trail.

"Oh my sweet Jesus," Henry said. "You got Lett Plunkett after you? What did you do to deserve that?"

Fargo said that he didn't know. "But I'm mighty tired of people trying to kill me. I'm just trying to do a job and earn my pay. No reason for anybody to be after me."

"That's where you're wrong," Rose said.

"How do you know?"

"When four people have tried to kill you in one day, there's a reason. You can bet on it. What's this job you're talking about?"

Fargo didn't say. Seth Rogers had made it clear that he was in a hurry to get his stage line started before anyone else did, and he wouldn't have wanted Fargo spreading the word about his plans.

"I didn't mean to be prying into your business," Rose said. "You don't have to tell me if you don't want to." She looked at Henry. "Do you think you can patch the tub?"

"I reckon I can do that. No shootin', though. I can't do that."

"Nobody wants you to do that. Mr. Fargo and I can take care of that. But if you can patch the tub, that would help. We get busy sometimes, and we need all three of them."

"All right." Henry looked down at the dead man in front of him, then turned to look at the one behind the chair. "What about them two?"

"Before you do any patching, you'd better go get the

36

sheriff. Tell him that two men tried to rob you, and you shot them."

"Ha! And you think he's gonna believe that?"

"He knows you work for me. He'll believe whatever you tell him. Go on now."

Henry stood up, shaking his head. "Somebody'll have to get Sloane."

"I'll send Bob over to get these two out of here. They'll be in the alley in back. Tell Sloane that Bob will help him move them later," Rose said.

Henry nodded and left, muttering "Goddamn" with every step.

"Who's Bob?" Fargo asked.

"He works for me. Does the heavy lifting that might be too much for a delicate flower of the West like myself."

Fargo didn't think Rose looked delicate—just the opposite in fact—nor did he believe a woman who carried a derringer and could shoot as accurately as Rose would need help with much. On the other hand, every saloon needed someone who could calm things down if they got too rowdy and bash in a few heads with a bung hammer if need be. Rose could probably wield a bung hammer with the best of them, Fargo thought, but she wouldn't want to clobber the customers herself. She was too much of a lady to dirty her hands—though she certainly knew how to shoot.

Thinking of Rose as a lady made Fargo smile. Rose said, "What's so funny?"

"Nothing. I was just thinking about something."

"And what would that be?"

"Never mind," Fargo said. He didn't think Rose would want to hear it. He strapped on his gun belt and took hold of the saddlebags. "Didn't you mention something about a drink and some talk before we got interrupted here?"

"As a matter of fact, I did. Follow me."

Fargo looked at the bodies. "Do you think it's a good idea to leave these two here without anybody around?"

"Don't worry about that. I'll send Bob."

Rose went out the back door of the room as Fargo followed. He didn't look back at the bodies of the two men that lay behind him, and he felt no regret for their deaths. They would certainly have felt none for him if they'd succeeded in what they'd planned.

Fargo and Rose walked down a short hallway that ended at a storeroom, the door partially ajar. Through the narrow opening, Fargo could see a shelf stacked with towels and bars of soap. A stove sat against the wall to the left, and on the opposite wall there was another door. Rose swung the door open and stepped through into the Lucky Lady Saloon, Fargo at her heels. Notes tinkled from an out-of-tune piano, playing a familiar song. Customers huddled around the gaming tables, and soiled doves laughed and flirted as they worked the floor, looking for someone to take them upstairs for the kind of sweet, loving dalliance that resulted from a satisfactory cash transaction.

The building was roughly finished, and the long bar wasn't really a bar at all—just nailed-together boards on stanchions. There was no mirror behind it, only a long shelf lined with bottles. From where Fargo stood, all the bottles looked the same. The whiskey in them had most likely been cooked up by somebody with a still and aged as much as a week. A tapped beer keg sat behind the bar, but Fargo was sure the beer wasn't any better than the whiskey. That didn't seem to bother the customers, who were happily swilling down whatever the bartender poured into their glasses.

The floor was too rough for dancing, but that didn't keep several miners from trying. Several women danced alongside them, no doubt hoping to pick up a customer. One enthusiastic man stomped so hard that dust rose up from the boards around him. The soiled dove nearest him stepped lively to keep her feet from being trampled.

Lights shined through cracks in the walls where the boards gaped apart. Fargo figured the Lucky Lady would be mighty cold in the winter when the wind howled down off the icy mountaintops. That wouldn't bother the miners or the women, however, not if they had enough liquor to get them through the season.

At the end of the bar stood a man who was at least as big as Lett, but cleaner and more cheerful in appearance. Rose spoke a few words in his ear. He nodded and left through the door Fargo and Rose had entered. When he passed Fargo, he gave him a dark look but said nothing.

"What about that drink?" Rose said when she rejoined Fargo.

He nodded toward the bar. "Doesn't look like there's much room there."

Rose sniffed. "I don't drink that stuff anyway. It's strictly for the customers. I have a bottle in my room that I save for special occasions. Like when a man visits for some talk."

"Sounds fine to me," Fargo said, and Rose started making her way to the stairway across the crowded saloon.

As she passed among the miners, some of them called out to her, and she always had a smile and a word for them. Fargo could see why the Lucky Lady was so popular. None of the miners would ever get more than a word and a smile, but the fact that they got that much gave them the hope that there might be more for them if they ever got lucky and made the big strike they were all looking for. Many of them had an envious glance for Fargo as he walked by them.

Fargo walked behind Rose up the stairs, admiring the sway of her hips in the fitted dress. He found himself looking forward to their talk.

When they reached the landing at the top of the stairs, Fargo saw the row of doors that ran along it. Most of them were closed, which meant that someone was inside earning money for herself and the Lucky Lady. And someone else was inside paying that money for his pleasure.

"I run a nice place," Rose said, as if Fargo might have some reason to doubt it.

He nodded in agreement, and she led him to the end of the hallway. He could hear muffled sounds from behind the doors they passed, moans of pleasure that could even have sounded real to the miners if they'd had enough of the bar whiskey.

Rose stopped in front of an open door at the end of the hallway.

"This is my room," she said.

It was a large room, decorated with red wallpaper and flower vases. The wide, plush bed looked inviting after Fargo's long day.

"I like it."

"I'm glad you do," Rose said.

She took him by the hand, and they went inside. She closed the door behind them.

7

Rose lit a lamp and set it on a small sideboard.

While Fargo studied the layout, she took out a bottle of whiskey from the sideboard. In one corner stood a rocking chair and a washstand with a bowl and pitcher on top. Frilly curtains covered the windows. The opposite corner was hidden by a changing screen.

Rose splashed whiskey into two glasses and handed one to Fargo.

"You can put those saddlebags down, Fargo," she said. "Unless you're planning to give me a ride."

Fargo laughed and tossed the saddlebags on the rocking chair.

"I'd say you were mighty attached to those bags, Fargo. Could it be that whatever brings you to Denver City is in them?"

Fargo had been thinking about Rose Malone as they walked to her room. He'd been thinking about a lot of things. Such as how four different men had tried to kill him in less than twenty-four hours. He hadn't known any of the men, but they'd known him. There hadn't been any doubt about that. The question was, why had they been after him? For that matter, how had they known where he'd be?

He wasn't a rich man, so he wasn't worth killing for the money he was carrying, but he did have something that might have been worth money to someone who knew he had it. He had the maps he'd made of the proposed stage route, with all the way stations marked.

Something like that would be very interesting to anybody who was thinking of starting a stage line and competing with Seth Rogers and Thomas Luman. Fargo wondered if there was anybody like that in Denver City. If there was, Rose Malone could know about whoever it was. Women in her line of work had a way of hearing things, and they often knew more about the town they were living in than most of the other inhabitants—and they knew how to keep things to themselves. Rose Malone herself might even be the kind of person who was interested in starting a stage line. She was enterprising enough, as he could tell from the saloon and bathhouse.

Fargo saluted her with his glass and smiled. "I don't believe I've thanked you for what you did in the bathhouse. That was good shooting, especially with a derringer."

"A lady has to know how to take care of herself."

Now she was calling herself a lady. Fargo smiled, and to cover it he took a drink of the whiskey. It went down smoothly and landed in his stomach with an agreeable burning sensation.

"You don't know me, Fargo," Rose said, "and I don't know you. So I don't blame you for not trusting me."

Fargo started to say that he trusted her, but he decided there was no use to lie. Rose was too perceptive for him to fool that easily.

"Would I trust you if I knew you?" he said.

"I don't know. But for what it's worth, I'll tell you my story." Rose took a small sip of whiskey and set her glass on the sideboard. "While I'm talking, I'm going to make myself comfortable. You move those saddlebags out of the way and have a seat."

She disappeared behind the screen. Fargo didn't think she was modest. He figured she just wanted to get rid of the derringer and whatever other weapons she might be carrying without his seeing where she hid them.

Fargo did as she'd suggested, moving the saddlebags to the floor and taking their place in the chair. It creaked a little when he sat down, but it was comfortable, and he allowed himself to relax.

"When I was a girl," Rose said from behind the screen,

"I wasn't like all the others I knew. All they could talk about was how they'd get married someday and have children. About living in a little white house somewhere with flowers out front and a husband who'd take care of them and earn a living. My family wanted the same thing for me, of course. That's what everybody wanted for their daughters."

While she talked, Fargo could hear clothing rustling as it was unfastened. He felt a pleasant tightening in his groin.

"I thought that sounded like a terrible way to live," Rose said. "I couldn't imagine wanting to be taken care of. I thought I could do a pretty good job of taking care of myself."

"You sure proved you could to me," Fargo said.

"I've had to prove it to a lot of others from time to time. But I made my own way, and I never had to ask any man for help. There aren't many women who can say that."

Fargo heard her slither out of her dress.

"You seem to have done all right for yourself."

"I've done just fine. This place might not seem like much to you, but it's bringing in a lot of money, even more than the one I was running in Kansas before the gold strike here. One of these days I might even get out of this business and settle down. I have enough money to do that, but right now I enjoy what I'm doing too much to quit. I treat my girls right. They can leave any-time they want to or think they have enough money to go out on their own, and that's fine. I make the custom-ers treat them right, too. Nobody lays a hand on them, and if anybody tries, they have Bob to deal with."

Fargo took the last sip of whiskey and set the glass on the floor beside the rocking chair. "Bob seems to like you."

Rose laughed. She had a nice laugh, Fargo thought, deep and throaty. It was a laugh you wouldn't get tired of.

"Bob likes me all right, but I don't sleep with the help any more than I sleep with the customers. I think Bob has the idea that one of these days I'll get desperate and invite him up here for a tumble, but it's never going to happen. There are too many complications that can come out of something like that. One of these days he'll get tired of waiting, and then he'll quit. But I'll find somebody to take his place."

"You're a practical woman," Fargo said.

"That's the truth. And what's your story, Fargo? How did you get from wherever you started to here?"

"I was just a kid with an itchy foot. Wanted to see what was on the other side of the hill, and then on the other side of the one after that. One hill just sort of led to another till I'd been down a lot of trails."

Rose stepped out from behind the screen. She wasn't wearing a stitch. Fargo stood up. He wasn't the only thing that rose.

"Like what you see?" Rose asked. Then looked down below his belt and gave her throaty laugh again. "Yes, I can see that you do."

Her breasts were large but firm, tipped with nipples already standing out, big as a man's thumb. Her skin was white and lightly freckled from the tops of her breasts to her shoulders. The hair that tangled at the V of her crotch was red as a flame.

"I think it's time for you to get out of those clothes," Rose said.

Fargo couldn't have agreed more. He pulled off his boots and dropped them in the floor, hung his gun belt over the back of the rocking chair, and stripped off his shirt and pants.

Rose gave him an admiring look and walked over to him. She took his stiff rod in her hand and gave him a light squeeze.

"I like a man who knows what he wants," she said, and ran her thumbnail along the underside of the tip.

Fargo trembled slightly, and Rose lowered her head to take him in her mouth. She took him deeply and began to make a purring noise deep in the back of her throat. Fargo felt the tension building in him, and the muscles tightened in his calves.

Rose released him and slid her tongue around the tip

44

of his straining erection before taking him in again. This time Fargo wasn't sure he could last, but Rose knew how to time things perfectly. Just before he reached the critical point, she let him go and stood up, smiling.

"I think it's time to move to the bed," she said, taking him in hand and leading him across the room.

When she reached the bed, she relaxed her grip and fell onto the mattress, sinking into it.

"Now let's see what you can do," she said.

Fargo lowered himself onto the bed beside her. First he ran his hand lightly over the stiffened nipples of Rose's breasts, causing a shudder to run down her body. Then he caressed one nipple with his tongue while continuing to run his hand over the other. After a few seconds, he let his hand roam lower, down the slight hill of her stomach to the flaming hair below. One finger slid into the slit between her legs and found it slick and ready for him. He waited for just a moment and then located her pleasure button, giving it a light touch. She shivered, and Fargo let his finger remain still as she moved her hips up and down.

She moved slowly at first and then with increasing speed. Before long she was moving both up and down and from side to side, sometimes, it seemed to Fargo, in both directions at once. His finger slipped over the slick button and into and out of her glory hole as she flung herself about with abandon. The bed was shaking so much that Fargo thought the rickety saloon might collapse as if an earthquake had struck it.

But if Rose had known when to quit with Fargo, she knew even better when to quit with herself. The motion of her hips gradually slowed, and soon she lay still.

"I'm ready for you now, Fargo," she said.

Her exertions had excited him, and he was more than ready to oblige. She spread her legs, and he entered her. He didn't use subtlety but plunged his whole length into her, the hair at the base of his rod tangling with hers.

They paused like that for a second, locked together, looking into each other's eyes, and then Rose began to move.

If her movements before had bordered on the frantic, they were now more controlled but no less exciting to Fargo, who found himself stimulated in ways that he had seldom experienced. It was as if all the feeling in his body had been concentrated in the tip of his tool, just waiting for the time to flood out in a white-hot rush. But he was determined to hold back until Rose had reached her own point of no return.

It wasn't long before she did. Her breathing grew faster, so much so that she was almost panting, and then she said, "Now, Fargo! Give it to me now!"

So Fargo gave it to her, in fiery bursts that came from somewhere down around the place where his toes joined his feet.

"Ahhhhhhhhhhhhh!" Rose said, wrapping her arms and legs around him and pulling him to her so tightly that he thought he might not be able to breathe.

She held him for a while as waves of pleasure convulsed her, and each wave drained a little bit more of Fargo.

Slowly the heaving beneath him subsided. After a while, she released her hold with a deep sigh of satisfaction, and Fargo rolled onto his back beside her.

"I knew you'd be good, Fargo," she said, a little breathlessly. "But I didn't know you'd be *that* good."

"I do my best."

"I hope you do it more than once."

"I think you can count on that," Fargo said.

"Oh, I am. In fact, I'm counting on it so much that I'm sure we'll be doing it again very soon."

"How soon?" Fargo asked.

"As soon as you're ready. How long will that take?"

As it turned out, it didn't take very long at all.

8

After a second go-round with Rose, Fargo put on his pants. Then he sat in the rocker and rolled a smoke from the makings he carried in his shirt pocket. He struck a lucifer with his thumbnail and lit up. He waved his hand to put out the flame, and inhaled, dropping the dead match into the whiskey glass on the floor. The smoke bit into his lungs, and he blew it out slowly. He thought about Rose and wondered just how far he could trust her.

There was no way to know for sure. But if he was going to find out why people were out to kill him, he'd have to trust someone, at least to a certain extent, and it might as well be Rose. She might be trying to kill him, but he liked the method she was using a lot better than any of the others he'd ever encountered.

"You asked me about my saddlebags," he said.

Rose was still lying on the bed with a sheet pulled over her for modesty's sake, though Fargo couldn't figure out what she had to be modest about at that point.

"You must have something valuable in them," Rose said, "otherwise you'd just have left them with your horse, which I suppose is at Carver's place."

"That's where he is. But I didn't want to leave the bags there. I have a few things in them that I don't want to get too far away from."

"You don't have to tell me what they are."

Fargo hadn't planned to do that. His trust extended only so far.

"What I'm carrying isn't important. But I want to ask you a question."

"Go ahead. But I think you already know all about me."

"This isn't about you. It's about someone else."

"Who?"

"That's what I'd like to find out. It would be someone who might want to start up a stage line between here and Leavenworth. Do you know anybody like that?"

Rose rolled up on her side and looked at him. "I don't suppose it's any of my business why you want to know."

Fargo took a drag on his cigarette and nodded to indicate that she was right.

"Then I won't ask. But I can't tell you the answer, either," Rose said. "It sounds like a good idea, and it might even pay off, but I haven't heard anything about it. You could ask Jonah Clark. He might know."

"Who's Clark?"

"He buys and sells gold claims. Among other things. He's not a regular customer here, but I've heard about him. He likes making money almost as much as I do, and he has his hand in a lot of different things."

"He sounds like someone I might want to meet," Fargo said. He thought it might not be necessary, however. If whoever wanted him dead was after the maps, it was too late to get them. Tomorrow, they'd be in the hands of Thomas Luman, and then it would be Luman who'd be in danger. Fargo figured that was Luman's problem.

"Clark has an office down the street," Rose said. "You could meet him in the morning."

"That should work just fine. I wasn't planning on going anywhere tonight."

"Oh. And what did you have in mind?"

"I think you know. But I can show you if you don't."

Fargo pinched out his cigarette, dropped the butt in the glass, and stood up, removing his pants.

"Oh, my," Rose said. "I do believe I know exactly what you have in mind. And the funny thing is, I was thinking of the same thing."

"Good," Fargo said. "I like it when everybody agrees."

And he walked over to join her on the bed.

When Fargo woke up the next morning he was momentarily disoriented. It had been a long time since he'd spent a night under a roof and in a bed.

The sun was already well up in the sky, which was another surprise. Fargo had never been one to linger when it came to getting up in the morning. But considering the fact that the previous day had been a long one, that four men had tried to kill him, and that he'd spent most of the night enjoying the energetic exertions of Rose Malone, he thought he could be forgiven for having slept a little longer than usual.

He got up and dressed. There was a mirror over the washstand, and after he'd splashed water on his face, he looked into the mirror and fingered the stubble on his chin. The shave he'd had the previous night would last for the day.

He was about to leave when Rose came in with a tray loaded down with a pot of coffee and a plate covered with ham and eggs.

"I thought you might want to eat something before you left," she said, setting the tray on the sideboard.

Fargo didn't like the domestic aspect of the situation, and he wished he'd left a bit sooner. However, he was indeed hungry, and the smell of the eggs and ham made him realize just how long it had been since he'd eaten. He appreciated what Rose was doing for him. Eggs didn't come cheap in a mining town.

"Don't worry," Rose said as if reading his thoughts. "It's just breakfast. I'm not trying to trap you or tie you down. I wouldn't like that any more than you would."

Fargo gave her a sheepish grin. "I appreciate the food. I can use it."

He took the plate and sat in the rocker. He balanced the plate on his knees, and Rose handed him a knife and fork. He was grateful that she didn't tuck a napkin under his chin.

He was even hungrier than he'd realized and polished off the plate of food quickly. After he'd thanked Rose for bringing it, he told her that he had to leave.

"Are you going to see Jonah Clark?"

"Maybe, but I have something else to do first," Fargo told her.

"Well, you feel free to drop by and see me any time you want to. It's not often that I meet a man like you, Fargo."

Fargo thanked her again and told he'd be back to see her before he left town. Then he picked up his saddle-bags and went to look for Thomas Luman.

Lett Plunkett didn't have a night like Fargo's. His cracked ribs throbbed so bad that he couldn't sleep, and he was cold in the night air. Having walked most of the day before, his feet ached almost as much as his wounds. His boots were fine for riding, but they weren't made for walking through the woods.

He spent most of the night up in the fork of a tree, hoping that some damned bear didn't climb up after him. Climbing up in the tree with his Sharps had been hard. Climbing down was even harder. With every move, Lett cussed the Trailsman and promised himself that he'd get even with the son of a bitch sooner rather than later. All he had to do was get himself back to Denver City, which was a lot easier to think about than to do.

But Lett was going to get there even if it killed him. And when he did, he was going to gut Fargo with his bowie knife.

The Gold Dust Hotel was the best place to sleep in Denver City. It was just about the only place in town where a man could get a room of his own. Most of the others required sharing, and if that was too highfalutin, there were always the canvas tents where a man could rent a cot for the night and sleep under a cover that kept off most of the rain, along with fifty or sixty other people who were trying to keep dry.

Fargo knew that Thomas Luman wouldn't be sharing any room, and he certainly wouldn't be sleeping under a tent with a bunch of snoring, snorting, farting miners. So Fargo went into the Gold Dust and asked the desk clerk for Mr. Luman's room number.

"And who wants to know?" the clerk asked.

He was a small man with a bushy mustache, little gold-rimmed glasses, and a wide gap between his two front teeth.

"I do," Fargo said.

The clerk looked up at him, started to say something, then didn't.

"Room eight," he said. "Down the hall on your right."

Fargo didn't bother to thank him. He went past the desk and down the hall. When he knocked on the door with the black 8 painted on it, a voice from inside said, "Who's there?"

"It's Skye Fargo, Mr. Luman."

Fargo heard movement in the room. The lock turned, and the door opened. It was held by a man in his forties, his eyes brown and clear, his hair combed, his clothing as clean as if it had been washed that very day. He looked like someone Fargo might have seen before, but he couldn't place him.

"I'm Thomas Luman," he said. "I'm pleased to meet you, Fargo. Won't you come in?"

Fargo stepped inside, and Luman closed the door.

"I wasn't expecting you quite so soon," Luman said.

"Mr. Rogers said you were in a hurry."

"Well, he was right. And we have good reason."

"I figured." Fargo unshouldered the saddlebags and set them on a chair. Pointing to them, he said, "Four men have already tried to kill me for what's in those bags."

"The maps," Luman said.

"That's right. The maps, not just of the trail but with the locations for twenty-seven way stations marked on them."

"It's valuable information," Luman said. "But we didn't think anyone would try to kill for it."

"Well, someone did. But it didn't do them any good."

"Naturally we'll increase your payment. We didn't expect you to have to deal with killers."

"I didn't expect to have to do it, either," Fargo said.

He opened one of the saddlebags and removed the maps that he'd drawn of the route from Leavenworth. Handing them to Luman, he said, "If I were you and Rogers, I'd get started on this thing today. Somebody's out to beat you to it, and there's still one of those killers on the loose somewhere."

"Only one of them?" Luman said, looking through the maps. He seemed more interested in them than in hearing about what had happened to Fargo.

"The other three won't be bothering you. One of 'em got away."

Luman folded the maps. "That's too bad. But you've done an excellent job here, Fargo, just the sort of thing Seth and I were looking for when he hired you. I'll go down to the telegraph office and let him know that you've arrived and that we have exactly what we needed. We'll get started on our stage line immediately."

"What about my pay?" Fargo said.

"I'll have to get the money from the bank. I'll do that this morning, and you can come back for it this afternoon."

Fargo didn't like waiting for his pay. When he did a job, he expected to be paid as soon as it was finished, but he didn't see any use in putting up an argument.

"I have a couple of things to do," he said. "I'll come back when I'm finished."

"That should be fine. I'll have the money for you then." Luman slapped the folded maps against the palm of his left hand. "You did a fine job, Fargo, and you'll get your money. You don't have to worry about that."

"I'm not worried about you paying," Fargo said. "But somebody wants those maps, and you might be the next target."

"Surely not. They wouldn't try anything in town."

Fargo wasn't as sure about that as Luman was, but he nodded his agreement. They shook hands, and Fargo left, hoping that Lett wasn't out there somewhere waiting for him. Or for Luman.

9

Fargo headed toward the livery stable to check on his Ovaro. He wasn't really looking for Jonah Clark's office. He figured that since he no longer had the maps, he wasn't in any danger from Clark, if that was who'd tried to have him killed, and he didn't hold a grudge since he hadn't been hurt.

He thought it might be a good idea to do something about Lett, but he didn't think Clark would admit to having hired him just because Fargo confronted him. Better to forget about the whole thing and get out of town. Maybe he could find somebody that needed a guide to Leavenworth, or up to Montana, or on out to California.

Or maybe he'd stay in Denver City for another night, considering the possible benefits. Going by to say good-bye to Rose would be the polite thing to do, after all. He could thank her again for the breakfast, not to mention other things. And if they did more than just talk, well, that would be just fine with Fargo.

The streets were noisy and crowded with miners pounding along the boardwalk, wagons creaking along in the street, and dogs barking. It took quite a noise to rise above all the others and call attention to itself. Occupied with his thoughts, Fargo might have walked right by Clark's office without even seeing it if there hadn't been a ruckus inside.

One man's voice rang out. "You sorry-assed son of a bitch! You'd as soon kill a fella and take over his claim as buy it from him. You sawed-off little bastard! I'm gonna take you apart with my bare hands."

Fargo stopped on the rough boardwalk and listened, as did several others.

"Sounds like old Elias to me," one man said. He spit a brown stream of tobacco out into the street. "Got a temper, that one has."

"Hell, I don't blame him," another said. "That damned Clark has stole more gold than any of the rest of us have found in Cherry Creek, and he didn't even have to work for it. If he's after Elias's claim, Elias had better keep a close watch on his back."

"Clark had to hire him some help to get those claims, though," the first man said. "Wouldn't dirty his hands to work a claim, and wouldn't dirty 'em to steal one, either, the son of a bitch."

Fargo got the impression that Clark wasn't the best-loved man in Denver City, but that was none of his concern. He might have passed on, but just then a man flew out of the door of Clark's office. His spread-eagled form cleared the boardwalk with ease and landed several feet out into the street, where he lay still.

A second later, a battered black hat sailed out into the street and landed beside him.

A man walked through the door who Fargo figured to be Jonah Clark. He was thin and elegant, dressed in dude clothes as if he were conducting his business somewhere in the East. He was clean featured, and most women would have called him handsome, though Fargo thought his eyes were a little too close together. Possum-eyed. Fargo never trusted a possum-eyed man, especially one dressed like a dude.

"I hope that will teach you a lesson," Clark said to the motionless man in the street. "You should never make accusations you can't back up with facts. If you do, someone might see fit to give you a thrashing."

Fargo found it hard to believe that the little man in the doorway had thrashed anybody, even the man who lay face down in the street, who looked considerably older and scrawnier than Clark.

54

"You couldn't thrash a rabbit," the man standing near Fargo said, spitting another tobacco stream.

Clark gave him a cold look. "I never said that I did," he told the man and stepped out onto the boardwalk.

He was followed by two men who were at least a foot taller than he was. They both had to turn sideways to get through the doorway.

Clark looked around at the crowd. "The fun's over here. Now why don't you loafers go on about your business and leave me to mine."

Fargo could hear some low mutterings that were uncomplimentary about Clark's ancestry and present condition, but people nevertheless began to move along.

Clark watched them go, nodded in satisfaction, and went back into his office. The two men stood on either side of the door for a few seconds, eyeing the crowd, before following him.

Fargo waited until they were back inside to step off the boardwalk and have a look at the fallen man in the street.

He struggled to a sitting position and put his hand to his head, feeling it gingerly. He took his jaw between his thumb and finger and waggled it back and forth.

"Guess I'm gonna live," he said after releasing his hold. "No thanks to that runty bastard." He cut his eyes at Fargo. "Mind helping me up, friend?"

Fargo offered his hand to the man, who reached over and picked up his hat and set it on his head. When he had it situated to his liking, he took Fargo's hand and pulled himself to his feet with Fargo's assistance.

He was a little shaky, and Fargo put a hand on his shoulder to steady him.

"Thanks," the man said, squinting out at Fargo from beneath his hat brim. "Do I know you?"

"I don't think so," Fargo told him. "Name's Skye Fargo."

The man extended his hand. "I'm Elias Shue. I work a little claim on Cherry Creek." He pointed at Clark's office. "And that son of a bitch in there is tryin' to steal it from me."

Fargo wondered what business that was of his, but before he could say anything, the two men who had thrown Shue outside came into the street. They strolled up to Fargo, stopping a few feet away to give him the once over.

Fargo stared back at them. The one on the right had lank black hair that hung down from beneath his hat, and a nose that had been broken a time or two. Part of one ear was missing, and the ragged skin made it look as if it might have been bitten off. His clothes were stained, and he smelled like a goat.

The one on the left grinned and showed that he had all his teeth, but they were yellow and crooked. There was nothing wrong with his nose, but the vacant look in his eyes made Fargo wonder if there might not be something wrong inside his head.

Fargo couldn't decide which of the two was bigger, not that it mattered much. Both of them were bigger than Fargo.

"Barker," Shue said, nodding to the one on the right for Fargo's benefit. "The other one's Toby. They whip people's asses for Clark, or whatever else he tells 'em to do. If he says *froggy*, then by God they jump."

Barker reached out a long arm and poked Shue in the chest with a finger the size of a cigar.

"You shut your mouth, old man. Or else Toby and I'll shut it for you."

"Yeah," Toby said, nodding.

Shue backed up a step.

"And you," Barker said to Fargo. "Who the hell are you?"

"Just somebody who's passing through town," Fargo said.

Barker extended his arm as if he were going to poke Fargo in the chest, but the Trailsman shoved the arm aside. A crowd had started to gather on the boardwalk, but Fargo paid them no mind.

"You don't want to do that," he said to Barker.

"You don't tell me what to do, asshole. I decide that for myself."

"Yeah," Toby said, his head still nodding from the last time he'd said it.

"You can't come around here and interfere in Mr. Clark's business," Barker said. "He don't like that. So you just move on along, and we'll see to old Elias here. We can take care of him better'n you can."

"Yeah," Toby said.

Barker reached out and put a hand to the side of Toby's head, leaving it there to stop its side-to-side motion.

"Stop that goddamn nodding."

"Yeah," Toby said.

Barker moved his hand and the nodding started again.

"To hell with it," Barker said.

He moved his hand and swung it backhanded at Fargo's face.

Fargo had been expecting something like that. He ducked under the swing and came up straight. Barker was half-turned around by the momentum of his swing, and Fargo put his boot into Barker's backside.

Before Barker could recover and turn back, Fargo gave a hard shove that sent the big man stumbling down the rutted street. His boot caught in one of the ruts and he fell, causing general laughter among the men who had stopped to watch the fun.

Toby grabbed Fargo's shoulder, spun him around, and swung at his head with a fist the size of a saddle.

Toby was big, but he was as slow physically as he was mentally. Fargo blocked the blow and punched Toby in the belly, which turned out to be taut as a drumhead. Fargo's fist bounced back at him. Toby grinned and swung again.

Fargo leaned back and let the punch sail by his face. He wasn't going to waste time trying to fight somebody who was hard as a rock and had the constitution of a mule—he kicked Toby hard in the balls.

Toby's eyes bugged out. He screamed and clutched himself, looking as if he couldn't believe what had happened. He sank to his knees, tears running from his eyes.

"Son of a bitch got what he deserved," Elias Shue said. Then, looking past Fargo's shoulder, he said, "Uh-oh."

Fargo turned just in time to see Barker charging

toward him. He had no time to brace himself, and the big brute slammed into him like a locomotive engine, encircling him with his arms.

Locked together, they fell to the street, Barker on top, his arms tightening their grip on Fargo as the man dug the toes of his boots into the ground and tried to squeeze the air from the Trailsman's lungs.

Nobody in the crowd was inclined to help. They might not have liked Clark, but they didn't want to get on his bad side.

Shue tried in vain to pull Barker off of Fargo. He might as well have been pulling on Pikes Peak for all the good he did. Barker didn't budge, and his grip didn't loosen.

Fargo had managed to keep one arm out of Barker's grip, and he put the heel of his hand under Barker's chin and pushed upward as hard as he could.

Barker's neck muscles strained, and his head moved about as much as an oak tree would have if Fargo had shoved it.

He was having difficulty breathing, and Barker squeezed tighter, so Fargo crooked his first two fingers and stuck them into Barker's nostrils. Barker tried to snort them out, but that didn't work. Fargo yanked upward, trying to rip the nose right off of Barker's face.

This time Barker's head moved back, and Fargo kept pulling. For all he knew he might have been successful at removing the nose, but about that time Shue took Barker's pistol out of its holster and hit Barker behind the ear with the barrel.

Barker was stunned, but not out. Shue hit him again, and Barker's grip on Fargo relaxed. He slumped forward. Fargo shoved him aside and rolled out from under him.

The Trailsman dusted himself off and looked over to see Toby still kneeling in the street clutching his crotch. Barker wasn't moving, and wasn't likely to for a while.

"I appreciate your help," Fargo told Shue.

"Hell, you wouldn't have been in that fight if it hadn't been for me. I'm the one who ought to be thankin' you."

He tossed Barker's pistol down beside him. "I take it that you're no friend of Jonah Clark's."

Fargo didn't want to go into his possible connection to Clark. He said, "I don't know the man. Never saw him before he came outside a while ago."

"Why'd you help me, then?"

"People have helped me from time to time. Every now and then I return the favor."

"You here to do some minin'?"

"I'm just passing through town."

"Lookin' for a job?"

"Depends on the kind of job," Fargo said.

"I could use a little help at my claim. Not that I need any protection or anything. You don't need to go thinkin' anything like that. I'm not afraid of Clark and his hired hands."

To prove that he wasn't just bragging, Shue toed Barker with his boot. Barker stirred, and the smaller man jumped as if he'd stepped on a rattler. Barker shook his head and moved himself up onto his hands and knees.

"We better get on down the street," Shue said. "Nothin' more we can do here."

Fargo grinned and nodded his acknowledgment. He looked over at Toby, who had rolled over onto his side, his hands still clasped over his family jewels.

"I need to go check on my horse," Fargo said. ".It's down at Carver's livery stable."

"I'll walk on down there with you," Shue said. "We can talk about that job."

Fargo didn't think he wanted a job working a gold claim. In spite of what Shue had said, he was pretty sure that what he'd actually be doing was providing protection for the old man. That generally wasn't Fargo's kind of work. But it wouldn't hurt to let Shue keep him company while he checked on the Ovaro.

"All right," he said. "You can talk, and I'll listen."

"Talkin's what I'm good at," Shue said. "That and findin' gold. I think you and I are gonna get along just fine, Fargo."

10

Carver had taken good care of the Ovaro, and Fargo told him that he'd be in town for at least one more day. The stable owner wanted to know how that would affect their deal for the other two horses. Fargo told him not to worry.

Fargo left the livery stable, Shue at his side, still filling his ear with the details of what a fine claim he had on Cherry Creek and how that low-down bastard of a Jonah Clark was trying to take it away from him.

"He tried to buy it fair and square," Shue said, "which is just fine. A man's got a right to do that. But I turned him down flat. That's when he started to get nasty. Said if I didn't sell to him, I might wind up dead in the creek some day. And that ain't the worst of it."

Fargo didn't want to hear the worst of it. It wasn't any of his business. "I have to go by the Gold Dust Hotel for a minute to do a little business. It's been a pleasure to meet you, Mr. Shue."

"Call me Elias. You mean you're not thinkin' about comin' to work for me?"

"I'm not cut out to be a miner," Fargo said. "I like being on the trail."

"Hell, minin's like bein' on the trail. Practically the same thing. Sleep out under the stars ever' night if you want to. You wouldn't have to, though, not at my claim. I got a solid little shack that I built myself. Cracks all chinked against the cold and ever'thing. Good as the Gold Dust, if that's where you're stayin'."

Fargo wasn't staying at the hotel and didn't plan to. If

Rose Malone didn't make him a better offer, he'd hang around the saloon and see if he could find somebody wanting a guide. If nobody did, Fargo would get back on the trail to Kansas, or to wherever it seemed like a good idea to go. There was nothing to hold him in Denver City.

As they passed a mercantile store, a woman came through the doorway. "It's about time you got here," she said to Shue. "You need to pay for our supplies so we can get back to the claim. If we stay away too long, Clark will have figured out some way to steal it from us."

"You don't have to worry about any stealin'," Shue said. "Me'n Fargo here have taken care of Clark and his bullyboys. Ain't that right, Fargo."

"Yes, ma'am," he said, looking the woman over. She was young, nowhere near Shue's age, and pretty. She had bright blue eyes, dark black hair, and a sensual, wide mouth. She was wearing a man's hickory shirt and loose-fitting denim pants, but they did little to hide a figure that would make a preacher kick over the altar rail to get at her.

"Fargo?" she said, eyeing him suspiciously. "I don't believe I know you."

"He's a fella that I'm tryin' to talk into helpin' around the claim," Shue said. "But he don't seem too interested."

"I'm interested," Fargo said, having suddenly changed his mind about the possible benefits of working a gold claim, or at least a claim where this woman might have an interest.

"Well, now, ain't that somethin'," Shue said. "Fargo, this is my daughter, Ruth. Like in the Bible. Here she is in the alien corn."

He touched the brim of his hat and said, "Pleased to meet you."

Ruth smiled, showing dimples that made her even prettier. "I'm pleased to meet you, too, if you were any help to this cantankerous old coot. He's going to get himself killed if he doesn't watch the way he talks to Jonah Clark."

Shue laughed. "Killed? You should've seen the way

Fargo and I cleaned up on Barker and Toby. They didn't know what hit 'em."

"I'm sure they didn't," Ruth said. "But right now you have to pay for our supplies or Mr. Gover is going to get upset with both of us."

"He can wait. How about it, Fargo? You gonna work for me at my claim?"

"I'll think about it. But I still have to go to the hotel and finish my business."

"That's fine. You do your thinkin', and we'll load up our wagon. You can meet us back here when you're finished."

Fargo said he'd do that, and left them there. He could feel those blue eyes on his back for a long way down the boardwalk.

The desk clerk at the Gold Dust was the same one Fargo had encountered that morning. This time he hardly bothered to look up when Fargo came into the hotel, and Fargo went on back to room number eight.

He was surprised to find the door slightly ajar, and when there was no answer to his light knock, he pushed it all the way open.

Luman was sprawled across the bed. For a moment, Fargo's pulse jumped. He went over to the bed and shook Luman's shoulder. After a moment, the man groaned. There didn't appear to be any wounds on him, so Fargo went back to the front desk and told the clerk to send for a doctor.

"What's the trouble?" the clerk asked.

"Mr. Luman's been hurt. You better get a doctor in here quick."

"We don't have any good ones around here. Just a couple of drunks that used to work medicine shows."

"Get the best one you can. Sober would be best."

"Not likely," the clerk said.

He came out from behind his desk, and Fargo went back to Luman's room. Luman was stirring around a bit, and after a few seconds, he sat up on the bed with a little assistance from Fargo. He felt his head and winced.

"Somebody hit me," he said. "Have a look."

Fargo checked. There was a little knot on the side of Luman's head in back of his ear.

"Who did it?" Fargo asked.

"I didn't see anybody. I'd just come back from the bank with your money, and when I opened the door, somebody came up behind me and hit me."

Fargo's stomach sank. "Where is it?"

"I had it right with me," Luman said, looking around the room. "But I don't see it anywhere."

The clerk came back then with a man who looked more like a miner than a doctor. He smelled of cheap whiskey and was carrying a worn leather bag.

"This here's Doc Ransome," the clerk said. "What's going on?"

"Somebody hit me," Luman said. "I think I've been robbed."

"The hotel isn't responsible for your personal goods," the clerk said. "If you were robbed, it's not our fault."

"Get outta the way," Ransome said. "Let me have a look at this fella."

Ransome was none too clean, but he seemed to know what he was doing. He examined Luman's head, checked his pupils, and asked about his vision. When he was done, he pronounced Luman fit.

"Just a little knock on the noggin. Nothing a dram of whiskey wouldn't cure." He glanced around. "Does there happen to be a dram here, by any chance?"

"I don't keep liquor in my room," Luman said.

Fargo glanced at the clerk, who looked away.

"This happened in your hotel," Fargo said. "The least you can do is give the man a drink."

"Make that two," Ransome said.

"You heard him," Fargo told the clerk, who glared back at him but decided not to make an issue of it.

"Didn't even break the skin," the doctor said. "You're a lucky man, Mr. Luman, if all you lost was money. Money can always be replaced, but a man's skull is a delicate thing, and you only get one of them to last a lifetime."

"It was my money," Fargo said.

"How unfortunate. But surely Mr. Luman will make things right for you."

Luman nodded, winced, and said, "It will take a while. I'm sorry, Fargo."

Fargo was sorry, too. Now he had a definite reason to stick around Denver City, and he was glad that Shue had offered him a job. He was also glad that Shue had a pretty daughter, who could do a lot to make the job more interesting than it would have been otherwise.

The clerk returned with a bottle of low-grade whiskey and two glasses. He gave one to the doctor and one to Luman. He didn't offer one to Fargo. After he had poured the drinks, Fargo asked him how someone could have sneaked up behind Luman or gotten into his room without being seen.

"It's easy enough," the clerk said, taking no offense at the question. "There's a back door at the end of the hall, and it's not locked. Sometimes I have to go relieve myself in the privy out back. I'm never gone long, but there's no one at the desk during that time."

Fargo nodded. It didn't surprise him.

"You think I should call the sheriff?" the clerk said.

"No," Luman said after taking a drink of whiskey. "I'll go to his office and talk to him personally."

Fargo didn't think it would do any good. He was of the opinion that Sheriff Tank Olson couldn't find his butt with both hands, much less a robber, even if he were to bother looking.

"I'm sorry about this, Fargo," Luman said. "I should have been more careful."

"It's not your fault," Fargo told him, though he wasn't sure how true that was. "You didn't have any reason to suspect you might be robbed. Any ideas about who might have done it?"

"No," Luman said. "How could anybody have known I even had the money?"

Fargo didn't answer. Someone knew a lot about the business of Rogers and Luman, and the information had to be coming from somewhere.

"Any chance of another dram of whiskey?" Ransome

asked, smacking his lips as if he'd just downed some of Ireland's best rather than the cheap rotgut provided by the clerk.

The clerk just looked at him and corked the bottle.

"I'll try to have your money in a couple of days, Fargo," Luman said.

"What about the maps?" Fargo said.

"Damn," Luman said, as if he hadn't thought of the maps at all. "They were with the money. They must have been taken, too."

Fargo could hardly believe it. He'd spent weeks on the trail, shot it out with four men, nearly been killed, all for those maps. And now they were gone, along with the money he was supposed to have been paid for making them. He started to say that Luman was a stupid son of a bitch and that he should have put the maps in the bank vault when he went to get Fargo's pay. But it wouldn't have done any good. The maps were gone now, and Luman probably felt as bad about it as Fargo did.

"You'd better let Rogers know," Fargo said.

"I will, as soon as I can get to the telegraph office. He's going to be upset."

Fargo couldn't say that he'd blame him. Luman's carelessness had created a lot of problems for everyone, and the lost money wasn't the least of them. The maps, if anything, were even more important. Rogers could always come up with money, but the maps were a different story.

"Could you redraw the maps?" Luman asked.

Fargo thought that he could do it, but he said he couldn't guarantee anything. He had a good memory, especially for trails, but it wasn't perfect.

"Come by tomorrow," Luman said. "When I send the telegram, I'll ask Rogers what he thinks we should do."

"You'd better see the sheriff soon, too," Fargo said.

"I will," Luman said. "You don't have to worry about that."

But Fargo worried about it anyway.

11

Fargo rode out to the gold claim in the wagon with Shue and Ruth. They'd gone by the livery stable and picked up the Ovaro. Fargo thought he might need a horse, so the animal was tied behind the wagon.

Ruth sat on the wagon seat between the two men, and Fargo was aware of the warm pressure of her leg against his as Shue kept up a running commentary about the country they were passing through and the evils of Jonah Clark.

"He's a low-down, slimy operator," Shue said. "He'll do anything for money. There's nothin' wrong with a man tryin' to make money," Shue said, flicking the reins in a futile attempt to get the flop-eared mule pulling the wagon to walk a little faster. "I'm not against that. I like makin' money myself, and I'm doing just fine on my little claim. Ain't that right, Ruth?"

"You talk like you're doing it all yourself," his daughter said. "You're going to give Mr. Fargo the wrong impression."

Shue leaned forward and turned his head so he could see Fargo.

"Ruth works as hard as any man," he said, "but that don't mean she belongs out here in this minin' country. Minin's rough work, and it seems to me that women aren't cut out for it."

"I'm as tough as you are," Ruth said. "Maybe tougher."

"I'm not sayin' you ain't, but it don't seem right to have a woman workin' a claim."

Fargo had been wondering about that. Most miners, if they had a partner at all, worked with another man, someone they'd known for a while and believed they could trust. Or if there was another family member involved, it was likely to be a son. Mining was a tough business, one that most fathers would never consider bringing their daughter into.

Of course, the Cherry Creek strike had nothing to do with mining in the strictest sense. From what Fargo had heard, nobody had struck a vein of gold that required digging. People were panning or using cradles, but no one had an actual mine.

Everybody was looking for one, though. The theory was that the gold in the creek had to be washing down from somewhere, and that somewhere was what most miners hoped to find—the rich vein that was going to make their fortunes.

But not all of them were looking for the big strike. Many were satisfied with smaller claims on a creek that brought them some flakes every day and even a nugget or two now and then, enough to keep them in liquor, with a little left over for a card game or a round with a soiled dove at the Lucky Lady Saloon.

Some men, and it was possible that Shue was one of them, even had enough sense to save their money and settle down eventually, while others went from one strike to the next, living from day to day and never thinking about what the future might hold beyond their next meal, their next drink, or their next woman.

Fargo sensed that Shue was likely to be more interested in saving his money because he had his daughter along with him. A daughter would be a serious hindrance to a man interested mostly in liquor and whores.

"He tried to keep me from coming along," Ruth said. "But I wouldn't listen to him. My mother died a year ago, and somebody had to take care of the cranky old codger."

"Now that ain't so, and you know it," Shue said. "I can take plenty good care of myself. Truth is, I couldn't leave you back in Kansas, because I was afraid you'd marry that Taylor boy and be ruined for life."

"There wasn't any danger of that," Ruth said.

"I should hope not. He was about as sorry as Jonah Clark. He was a banker, and you can't ever trust a banker or a man runnin' a medicine show wagon."

"We had a store," Ruth told Fargo. "Dry goods and hardware. Jeremiah Taylor was the banker who held the note on it. He wanted to court me, but my father was opposed."

"Didn't like that little sidewinder," Shue said. "Didn't trust him, either. And I was right, wasn't I? He wound up with our store, didn't he?"

"That was your fault. If you hadn't taken to the bottle after Mother died, it would never have happened."

Shue didn't say anything for a while after that. The only sound was the creak of the wagon and the occasional squeak of its wheels. Shue held the reins and looked straight ahead as they passed under the pines and cedars through which Fargo caught an occasional glimpse of the patchy blue sky.

After a while Shue started to talk again. "You're right to chide me about that drinkin', Ruth, and I don't blame you for it. I didn't know any other way to stop the hurtin' after your mama died, but all I did was cause more hurt to you, and myself besides. But by the time I figgered that out, it was too late to save my store." He leaned forward again and looked over at Fargo. "And that's why we're here in Colorado. I was flat busted and didn't see any way of gettin' any money to buy my store back or get another start. And then I heard about this Pikes Peak gold strike. I thought that might be my chance, and by God that thievin' Jonah Clark ain't gonna ruin it for me."

"We haven't found a lot of gold, Mr. Fargo," Ruth said. "But we've found enough to give us the hope that we'll find more. We're not here thinking we'll get rich. We just want to make enough to get us a new start."

The trail wound up a little hill, and when they reached the top, Fargo could see Cherry Creek through the aspens that grew along its bank. Shue turned the mule down a secondary trail, and Fargo saw a sturdy-looking cabin that stood near the bank.

"That's my claim," Shue said. "The one Jonah Clark would like to get from me. I've had my property taken away from me once by that damn' banker in Kansas, and it ain't gonna happen again. You can get a bet down on that, for sure."

Shue reined in the horses and hopped down from the wagon with an agility that surprised Fargo.

"You get Maggie unhitched, Ruth," Shue said. "Fargo can see to his horse while I carry the supplies in. Then we'll see if we can rustle up something to eat. Fargo's probably hungry."

"I had a big breakfast," Fargo said, thinking of Rose Malone and her hospitality, and wondering when he'd get a chance to take advantage of it again.

Shue had a corral in back of the cabin where Fargo led the Ovaro. There was a little chicken pen beside the fenced area and a small lean-to with a roost built under it, a couple of white hens scratching in the dirt and pecking at whatever it was they could find.

Ruth brought the mule back, and Fargo asked about the chickens while he rubbed down the Ovaro and grained him.

"They were my father's idea," she said. "He said we could save some money, and he was right. If we had to buy eggs, we'd have to leave off some other things we need."

When they returned to the front of the cabin, Fargo was carrying his saddle and saddlebags. Shue had the wagon unloaded, and he told Fargo to put his gear in the cabin. They went inside, and Shue located some dry bread and jerked beef, which they ate and washed down with water.

"We usually eat a little better than this," Shue said, " 'specially when Ruth has time to cook. You want to look over the claim, Fargo?"

Fargo agreed, so he and Shue went down to the creek while Ruth stayed behind to put away the supplies.

"I got a hundred feet along both sides," Shue told Fargo as they approached the creek. "That's the regular size of a claim here."

The water was flowing in the creek, though only swiftly enough to make some noise as it rippled over the rocks—clear enough for Fargo to see most of the way to the shallow bottom. The breeze rustled the leaves of the aspens, and Fargo thought that looking for gold might not be such a bad life. Although he would have preferred to have gotten his money from Luman and moved along, he might not mind so much spending a few days helping Shue.

"The thing about a claim is that you got to be here to keep it," Shue said. "If I was to be gone for five days, or if I was to get killed, somebody else could take the claim."

"There's always Ruth," Fargo said.

"That's what worries me. If Clark gets me, he has to get her, too. I wouldn't be any great loss to the world, but I don't want my girl gettin' hurt on account of me."

He didn't say that he was hoping Fargo could help keep anything from happening to Ruth, but he didn't need to. Fargo knew what he meant.

"I'll do what I can," he said, "but I'm not going to be around here for long. As soon as I get paid what's owed me, I'm leaving Denver City."

"We never talked about your pay," Shue said.

"I'm not worried about that." Fargo gave Shue a short version of what had happened that day. "So when Luman pays me, I'll be leaving."

"Sounds like you got a screwin' to me. I wouldn't be surprised if Jonah Clark was mixed up in it some way or the other. That's just the kind of a fella he is."

Fargo had been wondering about Clark. If he was interested in starting his own stage line, then he might very well have been the one who stole the maps and money from Luman. Of course Clark wouldn't have gone to the hotel and tackled Luman himself. That wouldn't be his way. He'd have sent Barker or Toby, if they'd been able to do the job after their little run-in with Fargo.

Fargo thought carefully. He and Shue had gone to the livery stable after the fight, taking their time, and then they'd walked back toward the hotel. They'd stopped at the mercantile store to talk to Ruth for a few minutes. Toby might not have recovered in that length of time, but Barker would have. Clark could have sent him to deal with Luman. It was something to think about.

But Fargo would have to do his thinking at some other time, because at the moment, Shue was telling all about his gold-finding methods.

"We got us a puddlin' tub here," Shue said, pointing. It looked like just a larger version of a miner's pan, nothing more than a big, round, watertight barrel made of wood.

"You just put your dirt and clay off the creek bottom in there," Shue continued, "and puddle it up with a stick. If you're lucky, there'll be a little gold at the bottom when you're done with it."

"And what if you don't get lucky?" Fargo asked.

"Well, then, that's not the end of it," Shue said. "Then you go to the cradle."

Shue's cradle was leaning against a tree near the creek bank. It was a trough about six feet long, with a smaller box on top that had a bottom full of holes.

"You take your wash out of the puddlin' tub," Shue said, "and you dump it in here." He smacked the box with the palm of his hand. "Then you rock the cradle with this handle while somebody pours water over the wash. Or if you ain't got anybody, you can do it yourself. The water carries off the dirt, and the gold's caught in the riffle bars under this box."

"I've panned for gold," Fargo said, "but I never used a cradle."

"A cradle's a lot faster, but you still have to get out in the creek and dig the dirt. A man can get mighty cold doin' that, dependin' on the time of year, and I'm hopin' to have enough money to leave this claim by winter. Hell, that water's cold enough even now, comin' down off the mountains the way it does."

"You could sell your claim to Clark when you leave. That should make him happy."

"I told him that, but he don't want it when I leave. He wants it now. Says it'll be played out by the time I get done with it, either that or somebody'll find the mother lode upstream from me. If that happens, they'll mine that vein without leavin' anything for me to find."

Fargo knew that could happen, but he didn't see why Clark was in such a rush to take just one man's claim.

"It ain't just me he's after," Shue said. "Clark's the kind of man that can't be happy with just a little somethin', like I am. He's gotta have it all. He's buying all the claims he can, up and down the creek. And what he can't buy, he takes, one way or the other. You saw what Barker and Toby are like. Not ever'body can stand up to 'em like we did. They've jumped enough claims along this here creek to make Clark a rich man."

Fargo asked what Toby and Barker did exactly.

"Well, they ain't killed anybody that I know of, but it ain't been for the want of tryin'. Luke Haberson had a claim downstream from me, and he got both his arms broke. He said it was from a fall, but ever'body knew better'n that. And then Ray Tolliver, upstream a ways. Said a horse kicked him in the head, but if I know Toby and Barker, it was one of them laid a pistol barrel upside it." Shue slapped the side of the cradle. "I wish to God I'd hit that Barker a little harder today."

Fargo thought it would be a good thing for Shue to get some permanent help around his claim. And there was Ruth to consider. Fargo might have to stick around a little longer than he'd planned for. He'd see what happened with Luman first, and then make up his mind.

"We've still got plenty of daylight left," Shue said. "What do you say we see if we can find a little gold?"

"Who's going in the creek?" Fargo asked.

Shue laughed. "I'll do that. I'm used to it."

"Let's give it a try, then," Fargo said.

12

Fargo and Shue put in a good afternoon's work with the puddling tub and the cradle, and by the time they called it quits, Shue was satisfied with what they'd found. No nuggets, but they hadn't really expected to get that lucky. There were enough flakes and dust to make the work worthwhile.

"Part of it's yours, Fargo," Shue said. "You done the work, so you deserve a share."

Fargo told him they could settle up later, though he didn't really intend to take any of the gold. He was building up a lot of credit in Denver City, he thought, what with the horses he'd be selling to Carver, the money owed to him by Luman, and the gold that Shue was trying to press on him.

The afternoon shadows were lengthening, and Fargo knew that Shue must be cold in his wet clothing. Fargo, whose job had been to pour the creek water into the cradle, was also wet and uncomfortable.

"We better get on back to the cabin and dry off," Shue said. "Ruth's prob'ly cooked us up some supper by now, too."

Fargo was surprised at how hungry he was. Working a gold claim sure did build up the appetite.

When they got to the cabin, he could smell fried bacon before Shue even opened the door. There was cornbread, too, and beans. They dried off quickly and sat down to eat. All in all, it was as fine a meal as Fargo could have hoped for, and, as he told Ruth, a more than adequate payment for the work he'd done that day.

After they'd cleaned off the table, Shue said he'd take the dishes down to the creek to wash them.

"Ruth does the cookin'," he told Fargo, "and I do the cleanin' up, as is only right."

Fargo offered to help, but Shue said that he could handle it. "You and Ruth can stay here and get acquainted. Two young folks like you ought to have something to talk about without an old fella like me around."

Fargo looked at Ruth, who colored slightly and didn't meet his eyes.

"You could show him some more of the claim," Shue said, but that wasn't what Fargo wanted to see more of, and he thought Ruth knew it.

"All right," Ruth said. "Come along, Mr. Fargo, and I'll show you what we have staked out here."

Shue gathered up the dishes and headed for the creek, and Ruth led Fargo in back of the cabin.

"You've already seen our chickens, Mr. Fargo. We gather the eggs every morning."

"Most people call me just plain Fargo and forget the *Mister* part."

Ruth continued to look at the chickens. "I don't feel I know you that well."

"We could take care of that."

She turned then. "I'm not sure what you mean."

"Well, we could do what Elias suggested. We could get acquainted. You could tell me about that Taylor fella, for one thing."

Ruth shook her head. "You don't want to hear about him. Come along, and I'll show you a bit more of the claim, but we shouldn't go too far."

Fargo followed her around the little corral. The sun had dropped behind the mountains, but there was still a reddish glow in the sky.

"What are you worried about?" Fargo asked.

"I'm not really worried, but it's nearly sundown, and it's not a good idea to get too far away from the cabin after dark."

"Elias mentioned something to me about claim jumpers."

"I'm not worried about them. Not if you're here. My father told me about what happened in town today."

"We had a little dustup, if that's what you're talking about, but Elias helped me out. I couldn't have handled those two rowdies without him."

"That's what I was talking about, but I think you're exaggerating. I know my father. He's a big talker, but he wouldn't be much help in a dealing with Toby and Barker."

"He did just fine. Laid Barker out flat." Fargo grinned as he thought about it. "If you're not worried about them, what's on your mind?"

"There are wild animals around here," Ruth said. She shuddered and not just because the evening air was taking on a chill. "We've seen bears."

Fargo knew about bears. He'd been worried about one only yesterday when he'd been taking cover from Lett and Red's bullets. One thing that drew bears was food, and Fargo figured the smell of bacon would still be on both him and Ruth.

He looked around. They were already a good way from the cabin. He could hardly see it in the dim light among the shadows of the trees, and it was going to be even darker in just a few minutes.

"You've a right to be worried," he said. "We'd better get on back. This is mighty pretty country, but we can talk just as well in the cabin as we can out here."

They turned around and started back, but they'd gone only a few steps when Fargo heard something rustling around back in the trees.

Ruth heard it, too.

"What's that?" she said.

"Probably a rabbit," Fargo said. "Let's get on along."

They didn't get far. The rustling got louder, and a black bear broke out of the trees about thirty yards in front of them.

Fargo stopped dead in his tracks and grabbed Ruth's hand. Chances were good that if they didn't move at all, the bear wouldn't even notice them. The light was bad, and bears didn't see all that well.

But they sure could smell. The bear stopped and shook its head, sniffing the air.

Fargo hoped the bear was a female. If that was the case, she'd likely have cubs at this time of the year, and her first instinct would be to run them up a tree and station herself at the trunk to fight off anybody crazy enough to get closer. And Fargo wouldn't get any closer. He'd go in the other direction.

The bear reared up on its hind legs, and it became obvious that it wasn't a female.

Fargo felt Ruth trembling beside him.

"What do we do now?" she whispered.

"We stand here and hope he's not interested in us."

She didn't seem to like the idea of staying there. "Shouldn't we run?"

"Worst thing we could do. Bears might look big and clumsy, but they can outrun a horse going up a hill or going down one."

Ruth looked around them. "We could climb a tree."

Fargo would have smiled if the situation hadn't been so serious.

"That bear can climb better than you can. He'd have you down from a tree in a second or two."

"You could shoot him."

"My pistol wouldn't bother him a whole lot from here. Not much more than a flea would. If he gets close, I might have to try shooting, but not yet."

The bear dropped down on all fours and turned toward them. Fargo had been afraid that would happen. It was time to consider getting out of there. Trouble was, he didn't know how they could do that without attracting even more attention than they already had.

The bear sniffed the air one more time, then started walking in their direction. He wasn't in a hurry, but Fargo could see that he had a purpose in mind.

He squeezed Ruth's hand. "When I say the word, you run. Don't stop till you're back at the cabin."

"What about you?"

"I'll be the one who stops the bear and keeps him from coming after you."

"Can you do that?"

The bear broke into a shuffling trot.

"We're about to find out. Go."

Fargo gave Ruth an easy shove to get her started.

He didn't look to see which way she went or even if she'd left, because the bear was almost on top of him by that time. He jerked his pistol from its holster, but he didn't fire. A bullet into the bear's body wouldn't have stopped it. A cannon, maybe, but not a shot from a Colt. He'd have to hit it in the eye to kill it, and even that was chancy with the way the bear was moving its head around.

When the bear reached Fargo, it didn't knock him down. Instead it stopped and reared up on its hind legs again. It roared, showing the black lips that rimmed the red mouth and the white fangs set in the powerful jaws.

Fargo took a step backward, and the bear made a swipe at him with five claws that were sharper than a bowie knife. They shredded the sleeve of Fargo's buckskin shirt and bloodied his arm, but he didn't feel a thing. He would later, he knew, but now there was no pain at all.

The bear dropped back down, and Fargo hit the ground at the same time. He switched his pistol to his left hand and kept his bloodied right arm beneath him. He could use the pistol with his left hand if he had to, but hoped he wouldn't have to. He didn't move. He did his best not even to breathe.

The bear seemed a little puzzled. It stood for a while doing nothing, and then it came over to Fargo and sniffed at him. Fargo hoped that the bacon smell hadn't saturated his clothing the way it must have Ruth's. And that the blood smell wasn't strong enough yet to interest the bear.

He was about to find out. The bear stood over him and lowered its head to sniff him. When it exhaled, Fargo could feel its hot breath and smell its meaty stink.

Fargo remained still. He'd been told that bears weren't interested in you after you were dead, so the best way to escape an attack was to pretend that you'd died. He'd never put that to the test, and he'd never been sure that was true. Now he was going to find out. If he'd been lied to, he'd be dead without having to pretend.

The bear nudged him with its nose. Fargo was yielding but still. That kind of thing went on for a minute or two, the bear nudging and Fargo trying not to move. Fargo hoped the bear wasn't going to roll him over and find that bloodied arm. If it did, there was going to be real trouble.

Not for the bear. For Fargo.

Fargo had been in a tight spot or two in his time, and he knew how to wait, the way he'd waited for Red and Lett to come to him after they'd tried to kill him. But waiting for the bear to get tired of sniffing at him was one of the hardest things he'd ever done. He could feel his muscles knotting up from the tension.

Finally the bear snorted. It raised its head and looked around. It must not have seen anything interesting because it turned and ambled away.

Fargo watched it go. When it was out of sight in the trees, he got up and holstered his pistol, which was slippery with the blood that had run down his arm. He started down the trail to the cabin, and when he was about halfway there, Ruth met him.

"Are you all right?" she said, her voice filled with concern.

"You didn't go to the cabin," Fargo said.

"I went most of the way. I couldn't just leave you out there."

She'd gotten far enough away to be out of the bear's range, so Fargo didn't scold her. He said, "My arm's going to need some fixing. No telling what might happen when you've been clawed."

"We'll go to the cabin, and I'll clean the wound. That was the bravest thing I've ever seen."

"Or the craziest," Fargo said as they started back toward the cabin. "I wouldn't recommend it as a general practice."

"Why didn't you shoot him?"

"If you don't make the first shot, there won't be any time for another one. I thought I could stay still long enough to make him lose interest, and it worked out."

When they reached the cabin, Shue saw Fargo's arm. "Holy Jesus, Fargo, what the hell happened?"

Fargo told him as Ruth took him to the table and cut away the sleeve of his shirt.

"If it was me," Shue said, "I'd have laid that scutter out with a pistol barrel across the top of his head. Like I handled Barker."

"I didn't think of that," Fargo said. "But I don't believe it would've worked. A bear has a mighty hard head."

"Might have if you'd hit him hard enough, the way I pounded on Barker."

"Where's the whiskey?" Ruth said, interrupting Shue's bragging.

Shue turned to her. "What? You know we don't have any of that stuff around here."

"This is no time for that old story," Ruth said. "I know you don't drink anymore, but I also know you've got some whiskey around, just in case you took a notion. So where is it?"

Shue said nothing. Looking a little sheepish, he dug around behind the woodbox and came up with a bundle wrapped in a ragged blanket. He unwrapped the bottle and handed it to Ruth, who opened it and poured whiskey over Fargo's arm.

"Hate to see it used like that," Shue said, shaking his head while the whiskey burned its way into the deep scratches. "But it's prob'ly for the best. It'll clean that wound, and God knows I oughtn't to drink it. Not that I do. There's not a drop of it touched my lips since we left Kansas."

"And it never will, because I'm going to use all of it," Ruth said.

"Better not," Fargo told her. "You never know when you'll need it again for something like this."

Ruth admitted that he was right and sealed the bottle after using only a small amount on his arm. She handed the bottle to Shue, who wrapped it in the blanket.

Just before he put it back behind the woodbox, he looked at Fargo, gave him a wink, and said, "See? I told you the two of us were goin' to get along."

13

Fargo slept outside that night. Shue had asked him to stay in the cabin, but there was hardly room for Shue and Ruth. Fargo preferred the outdoors. The earthen floor of the cabin was harder than the ground outside, and besides, Fargo liked the smell of the pines and the sight of the stars through the trees. He insisted that the cool night air wouldn't bother him, and Shue didn't argue.

"You go on ahead," Shue said. "You know what's best for you. Are you sure that arm's gonna be all right?"

Fargo held up his arm for Shue to have a look. Ruth had dressed the wound and bound it with clean strips torn from a piece of an old shirt. The bleeding had stopped, and Fargo knew he wasn't in any danger of having the wound fester on him.

"It's fine," he said. "Be healed up in no time at all."

"Good thing. You'll need it to help me with that cradle tomorrow."

"I'll help you," Ruth said. "Fargo doesn't need to be using that arm for a while."

Fargo noted that she'd dropped the *Mister*, and he took that as a good sign. He told them he'd be just fine and not to worry about him. Then he went outside. He looked around for a likely spot and decided that he'd do best in back near the Ovaro and the chickens.

He found a place he liked under a tree and laid his bedroll down. He could hear the chickens stirring on their roost, occasionally clucking in their sleep, and the Ovaro whickered once to let Fargo know he was there.

The moon was full and bright overhead, casting shadows down through the trees. The air was brisk, and Fargo thought it would make for good sleeping. He'd had a long day.

He lay down, closed his eyes, and wondered what Rose Malone was doing. But not for long, and he was asleep before he had time to think about anything else.

He woke up with a start a bit later. How much later, he didn't know, but the moon had gone down, and it was so dark that Fargo might as well have been blindfolded. He felt for his pistol, which he'd put near his side, and relaxed a little when his hand closed around the grips.

"Fargo, are you here?" someone whispered.

Recognizing Ruth's voice, Fargo put the pistol down and said, "Right over here."

Ruth was having a little trouble finding him in the blackness, but eventually a dark shape appeared near him.

"A little to your left," Fargo said.

She found her way to where he lay and knelt down beside him.

"I thought my father would never go to sleep," she said. She laughed quietly. "All he could do was talk about how well you and he got along and how the two of you cleaned up on Barker and Toby today."

"Is he asleep now?" Fargo asked.

"Can't you hear him snoring?"

Fargo listened. He could hear a distant buzzing sound, gravelly and grating, as if someone were trying to shape a soft board with a rasp.

"That can't be him," Fargo said.

Ruth laughed again. "That's him. He's making enough noise to wake the dead, but it doesn't bother him. It just bothers anybody else who happens to be around. Once he gets to sleep, nothing can wake him unless it's a bucket of water in the face."

"Then I don't guess we'll bother him with our talking. Or anything else."

"No," Ruth said. "We won't."

There was a pause. Fargo said, "Was it too warm in the cabin?"

"No. I came out here to thank you for saving me from the bear."

Fargo smiled, though he knew she couldn't see him. "I didn't do anything except lie down."

"Yes, you did. You sent me away while you stayed there. If you'd tried to get me to lie still while that bear sniffed around me, I'd have screamed or done something else crazy. And we'd both be dead."

"You never know how things will work out," Fargo said.

"No," Ruth said. "You never do."

She leaned down and kissed him.

Fargo was never one to let an opportunity like that pass him by. He kissed her back, and their tongues met and tangled.

Fargo slid his hands up under her loose shirt and cupped her fine, firm breasts. The nipples hardened at his touch.

Ruth broke the kiss and raised up to take off her shirt. Fargo wasted no time in removing his own, and then she was pressed against him. They kissed again, her burning nipples searing his chest like a brand.

Again Ruth broke it off, this time to stand and remove her loose-fitting denims. Fargo got out of his pants at the same time and pulled her to him. His erect rod, hard as a bowie's tempered blade, was trapped between them, generating enough heat to power a steamboat up the Mississippi.

Ruth drew in a deep breath. "My God, Fargo."

They kissed again, and then sank down onto Fargo's bedroll. He took a stiff nipple into his mouth and sucked it in deeply. Ruth moaned and ground her hips against him. He slid his hand down her smooth belly until it encountered the rough hair at the base. She was dripping with readiness, and Fargo was just as eager as she was.

He spread her legs and knelt between them, allowing the sensitive tip of his stiffened shaft to touch her lightly just at the edges of her nether lips. She moaned again and took hold of his penis, working the tip of it rapidly up and down the slit, moaning loudly each time it touched just the right spot.

Listening to her cries increased Fargo's own excitement, and when she guided him into her, he was more than ready. She was as hot as a volcano and the slick lava that lubricated him seemed to pull him inside of its own accord. He began to move, slowly at first, and then faster as his pleasure increased. Ruth churned her hips wildly. Then she stopped suddenly, clasped his buttocks in her hands and pulled him hard and deeply into her. She held him there and began rotating her hips slowly, and it was as if someone were stroking the tip of Fargo's rod with a soft, hot hand. She sped up gradually, and then said, "Oh! Oh! OOOOOH!" Fargo knew it was time and jetted into her in a long continuous stream.

Fargo located his shirt, rolled a cigarette, and lighted it. He lay back beside Ruth and smoked contentedly.

"It had been a long time for me," Ruth said, almost as if she were apologizing. "And that was wonderful."

"You're right about that," Fargo said, even though it hadn't been a long time for him.

Ruth touched his cheek. "You're not going to stay with us long, are you?"

"Not likely," Fargo admitted. "I'm not the kind who stays in one place for very long at a time. I have a lot of things to get settled in Denver City, but when they're taken care of, I'll be on my way."

"You never told us why you were here. I know it's none of my business, but it's easy to see you're no miner."

"You're right," Fargo said. "I'm no miner. Even that life is too settled for me. I'm a trailsman. I'm a lot more at home on the trail than in a town, and I make my living by guiding, blazing trails, whatever I can find in that line of work."

"And you don't have any connection to Jonah Clark?"

Fargo had to think about that. There might be a connection, or there might not. If Clark was the one who wanted him dead and who'd stolen the maps and his money, then there was one. Otherwise, there wasn't.

"Not that I know about," he said.

He pinched out the cigarette and tossed away the butt. What really bothered him was the fact that he wasn't entirely sure that he was safe from attack even now that the maps had been stolen, presumably by whoever had wanted them in the first place.

And somewhere Lett Plunkett was still alive.

There was also the matter of Fargo's payment. Whoever stole the maps had also taken Fargo's money. If Clark was the guilty one, then there was a connection between them, after all. Luman had promised to get money from Rogers to make the payment owed to Fargo, but the Trailsman had heard assurances like that before. As often as not, they were as empty as a whore's sacred word.

If there was one thing Fargo knew for sure, it was that he wouldn't be leaving Denver City without his money, and whether he had to get it from Clark instead of Luman didn't matter. He'd do whatever it took.

He also felt a bit of an obligation to Shue and Ruth. He knew he didn't owe them anything, but he liked both of them, and they did need someone to take care of them. From what they'd told him, it was a wonder that Clark hadn't killed one or both of them already.

"Fargo?" Ruth said.

Fargo's thoughts had drifted a long way from the woman at his side, and he brought them back again.

"I don't want to die here, Fargo," Ruth said. "I don't want my father to die here, either."

Fargo wondered now whether her eagerness of a few minutes before had been as much a result of her desire as of her hope that she might tie him more closely to her and her father. It was probably some of both, but considering the heat of their lovemaking, mostly the former. Well, the truth was that in helping them out, he might be helping himself.

"I don't blame you," he said. "I'll be around for a while, and we'll see how things work out. It could be that I'll have to take care of Clark before I leave."

"I hope so. He's going to run all of us off this creek if he can, and so far nobody's really tried to stop him."

"What about the sheriff?"

Ruth gave a soft laugh. "Sheriff Olson's just another one of Clark's hired hands. Olson doesn't care what happens in Denver City, as long as Clark is happy."

Fargo had gotten the impression when he'd brought Red's body to town the previous night that Tank Olson didn't give much of a damn about being sheriff. Now he knew where the lack of interest came from.

Come to think of it, Olson had known who Fargo was. Not too surprising, maybe, since he'd be a lot more likely to know than someone like Ruth. Still, it made Fargo suspicious since Lett and Red had known him, and so had the two who'd tried for him at the bathhouse.

By now the heat generated by his encounter with Ruth had begun to leave Fargo's body. He put his shirt and pants back on, and Ruth got dressed as well.

"I'd better go back inside," she said. "I want to be there when my father wakes up in the morning. I hope we didn't do anything to hurt your arm."

"I didn't even feel it," Fargo said. "I was too busy feeling something else."

Ruth laughed, kissed him on the cheek, and left him there.

14

Fargo's arm was feeling fine the next morning, and he told Shue that he was going to ride into town.

"I have some business that has to be taken care of," he said. "If I get back here in time, I can help you work the claim later today."

"Ruth can help me," Shue told him. He didn't say that Ruth was as good as Fargo at the job, but the tone of his voice clearly implied it. "I just hope Clark don't send his ruffians out here to get rid of me while you're gone."

Ruth, who was standing nearby listening to them talk, didn't say anything, but she followed Fargo back around the cabin after he got his saddle.

"Do you think we'll have any trouble with Clark today?" she asked.

Fargo didn't answer. He put the blanket and saddle over the Ovaro's back, settled things to his satisfaction, and tightened the cinch. He took the bridle from a nail on the fence and fitted it on.

When he was finished, he looked at Ruth. "You don't have to worry about Clark for a while. He won't try anything so soon after Elias and I roughed up his men. That would be too brassy even for somebody like Clark, and people might not stand for it."

"I'm not so sure anybody would care," Ruth said. "Mostly, they look out for themselves. Will you be back tonight?"

Fargo knew what she meant, but he didn't like to make promises.

"You can bet I'll try to be," he said. "Stay away from bears while I'm gone."

He mounted the Ovaro, told her good-bye, and rode away. He looked back before he got to the main trail and saw her watching him through the trees.

"I tried to arrange something with the bank," Luman told Fargo. "But it's going to take a little time to get things worked out with Seth."

Fargo didn't like the sound of that. They were in Luman's room at the Gold Dust, and Luman looked none the worse for having been robbed and hit on the head.

"I told Seth that you deserved payment, even if the maps were lost," Luman said when Fargo expressed his displeasure. "You did your job, and it's not your fault I got robbed. But he says that without the maps, what you did doesn't matter."

"I did the job I was paid to do," Fargo pointed out. "You're the one who lost the maps."

"That's just the way I put it to Seth in the telegram, like I told you, but he's a hard man when it comes to business dealings. He said that if you could draw the maps again, that would be fine. Then I can pay you."

"That's just plain not right," Fargo said, knowing even as he did that there was nothing he could do about it. Seth Rogers was in Kansas, out of his reach, and Luman apparently couldn't get the money for the payment without Rogers's approval.

"All you have to do is draw those maps," Luman said. "They don't have to be perfect. Just as close as you can come. Seth and I will take care of the rest. You can use my room. I'll have a table brought in and get things set up. How about it?"

Fargo thought it was a bad deal all the way around, but he couldn't see any way out of it.

"You've got me in a bind," he said. "So I'll have to do it."

"Good. That's fine. I'll arrange for a table and some paper and pencils. You just sit down, and I'll be right back."

There was only one chair in the room, a rocker that wouldn't be any good for working.

"Get me a chair, too," Fargo said before Luman could get away. "A straight-backed one."

Luman said he'd do that and left the room.

Once again, Lett Plunkett hadn't had a night anywhere nearly as pleasant as Fargo's had been. While Lett hadn't encountered a bear, he hadn't encountered a beautiful woman who wanted to sleep with him either. He hadn't had anything to eat. His ribs still hurt him whenever he moved, and he had to move a lot since walking was his only means of transportation. Naturally he wasn't in the best of moods.

The only good thing about his situation was that he'd almost made it back to Denver City.

When he got there, the first thing Lett was going to do was have himself a steak, then a drink, and then, if the Trailsman was still around, Lett was going to kill him.

Lett wasn't one to think too far into the future, so he didn't much care what happened after that.

A man Fargo didn't know brought a table into Luman's room, left without a word, and returned with a chair. He was followed the second time by Luman, who had paper and pencils.

"You just take your time," Luman told Fargo. "I have some things to attend to, so I won't be here to bother you." He put a map on the table. "I brought this in case it might help you. It's not very detailed, but it has the two main trails on it, the Oregon and the Santa Fe. Maybe it will refresh your memory."

Fargo thanked Luman, who left without any further discussion. Fargo spread the map and the paper out on the table and picked up a pencil. It had already been sharpened.

Fargo sighed, sat down, and started to work.

He worked straight through the day, and, after a lot of wadding up paper and starting over, Fargo was more or less satisfied that he'd reproduced something that was pretty close to his original map. His memory for trails and landmarks was a lot better than most people's, but getting the locations of the way stations exactly right without any reference points was next to impossible.

Well, he thought as he laid the pencil aside for the last time, it was as close as he was going to get, and it would be better than no map at all. It would serve the purpose, unless someone else had already started building a road by the time Seth Rogers got it.

Fargo stood up and stretched. It was after noon and he hadn't had anything to eat. He wondered what had happened to Luman, and he knew one thing for sure: he wasn't going to leave the map he'd just drawn there in Luman's room without someone around to look after it. He folded it carefully and stuck it in his shirt.

The desk clerk didn't know where Luman was, either.

"He doesn't confide in me, and I try to mind my own business," the clerk said, as if to imply that Fargo should do the same.

"It's my business to know where he is," Fargo said. "He owes me money."

"His room's paid up, and that's all I care about," the clerk said, and Fargo left the hotel to find something to eat. There was a café set up under canvas not far away, so that was where Fargo headed.

Before he got there he could smell fried meat and coffee. He could use some of both. The tent flaps were tied back, and Fargo stepped inside to look around.

The place wasn't crowded at this time of day. There were a dozen men sitting at tables, laughing, talking, and eating. Knives and spoons clinked against plates, and everybody seemed happy, except one man who sat near the back of the tent, sawing at his steak with a bowie knife.

He looked up when Fargo came through the entrance. His eyes opened wide in recognition, and his mouth widened in a happy smile as he stood and threw the bowie knife hard. It flew end over end and straight at Fargo.

Fargo had recognized Lett at the same moment Lett

had recognized him, and he was already moving before the knife was on its way. He dived to the side, hitting the dirt floor and rolling under a table. The knife thunked into the shoulder of a man who'd been entering the tent behind Fargo. The man yelled in pain and surprise and fell back outside the tent.

Lett roared in frustration when he saw that he'd missed his target. He kicked the table out of the way and started toward the spot where Fargo lay. Ignoring the pain in his ribs, he knocked aside the tables, chairs, and benches that were in his path. The men who'd been eating so cheerfully and enthusiastically only moments before were jumping out of his way as their plates and food went flying.

Fargo came up from under the table with his pistol in his hand, but he didn't get a chance to use it as Lett brought a chair crashing down on his arm and hand. The chair shattered apart. Splinters and bigger pieces of wood went in all directions, and the pistol skittered away across the table.

The chair was followed by Lett, who jumped at Fargo with a bull-moose bellow.

Fargo fell back, and Lett landed on the table. The table legs collapsed underneath him, but on his way down, Lett stuck out a hand and grabbed Fargo's bandaged right arm.

Pain ran from the wounded arm straight up to Fargo's head, where it exploded behind his eyes.

Lett could tell that Fargo was hurting, and he intensified his grip on Fargo's arm as the two of them struggled on the ground, overturning tables, banging into chair legs, and churning up dust that got into Fargo's nose and mouth.

Fargo hardly noticed the taste or smell of the dust as pain shot through his arm. Lett was hanging on to it like a dog with a soup bone, straining as if he were trying to twist it off at the shoulder.

Fargo pounded Lett in the ribs a couple of times to give him something to think about, and Lett relaxed his hold long enough for Fargo to roll away. As he did, he knocked over a table that held a coffeepot. The coffee spilled out all over Fargo's chest and leaked inside his shirt. Fargo knew that the coffee wasn't doing the map any good, but he didn't have time to do anything about it.

He jumped up, knocking over another table and scattering the miners who had been standing there like a covey of frightened quail. They backed against the canvas side of the tent and tried to stay out of the way of Lett, who was on his feet by that time and flailing away at Fargo.

The force of Lett's attack staggered Fargo and sent him stumbling toward the rear of the tent and through the back flaps. There was a little cook shed located behind the tent, and Fargo slammed through the door into the stove, knocking it off the bricks that it stood on. Fargo wasn't burned, but sparks flew out of the stove and landed on his clothes where they burned small holes into the buckskin.

The cook tried to hit him with a big black skillet, but Fargo dodged it.

Lett didn't. He had followed Fargo into the shed just in time for the skillet to hit him in the middle of the forehead. The skillet rang like a gong, and Lett stood stock still, his eyes glazed.

Fargo hit him in the ribs again.

The blow woke Lett up. He grabbed a cleaver from a nearby chopping block and swung it at Fargo's head. If it had landed it would have split Fargo's skull, but once again Fargo was able to dodge the blow.

The cook, unfortunately, did not. The cleaver that missed Fargo took off the cook's hand at the wrist.

The skillet hit the ground, the cook's hand still holding on to the handle, and blood gushed from the stump of the cook's arm.

Screaming and waving his arm, the cook tried to run out of the shed. Lett shoved him out of his way, and blood spurted into Lett's eyes. While Lett pawed at his face, Fargo snatched a butcher knife from the cook's work area.

Lett, partially blinded by the blood, didn't know that Fargo had the knife, and he charged the Trailsman with the cleaver held high and ready to chop off whatever appendage he could get to. Fargo surged forward, sinking the knife into Lett's chest. Unlike the bullet that struck a rib, the knife went straight in and punctured the big man's heart.

Lett's brain didn't quite get the message that he was dead, and he swung the cleaver weakly. His arm draped over Fargo's shoulder, and the cleaver fell to the floor of the shack.

Fargo pushed Lett's arm away, then shoved him in the face with the heel of his hand.

He fell straight backward without bending, the way a tree falls, and hit the ground hard. Dust puffed up around his head.

Fargo wasn't sorry to see him dead. The only regret the Trailsman had about Lett was that now Lett wouldn't be able to say who'd hired him.

15

Fargo didn't waste any time on Lett. He had to do something about the cook before the man bled to death. He knelt down by the now unconscious man and ripped away a strip of the man's shirt to use as a tourniquet.

When he'd tied it tightly, a man who had come out of the tent to see the end of the fight said, "Better cauterize that stump."

"Be a good idea," another man said.

"You go get a doctor," Fargo said. "Another man got hurt, too."

"Yeah, that was old Franklin. He's all right. Pulled that knife out."

"I don't want a story," Fargo said. "I want a doctor."

"Well, you don't have to be so damned huffy about it," the man said as he stomped away. Fargo hoped he was going to find a doctor and not to sulk.

"Help me get the cook up," Fargo said to the man who remained, and the two men lifted the cook to his feet.

"They call me Muley," the man said.

He was young, not much over twenty, Fargo estimated, and didn't look quite as hardened as some of the miners in town.

"I'm Fargo," the Trailsman told him. "How are we going to do this?"

"The stove?" Muley said. "Prob'ly the best way for what I'm thinkin' you got in mind."

Fargo nodded. "Might as well."

They got the cook over to the stove, and Muley said,

"I'll try to hold him. You'll have to do the other. I don't have the stomach for it."

Fargo did, but all the same he was glad the cook had passed out. Even at that, what they were going to do would be hard on him.

"I got him," Muley said, taking hold of the cook with a bear hug around his chest. Blood was still running out of the stump of the cook's arm.

"Hang on, then," Fargo said.

He took hold of the cook's arm and pressed the end of it to the hot stove lid.

There was a harsh sizzling noise and the smell of burning blood and meat, while the cook thrashed and writhed like a man in the throes of Saint Vitus's dance. It was all Muley could do to hang on to him.

When it was over, the cook slumped against Muley, who dragged him over to a stool that sat against the wall. He lowered the cook to the stool and leaned him back against the planks. The cook's head lolled forward on his chest. The bleeding had stopped.

As Fargo was loosening the tourniquet he'd tied on the cook's arm, the doctor came to the front of the shed and looked down at Lett's body. It was Ransome, the same man who had seen to the bump on Luman's head.

"Seems like nothing I can do for this fella," he said, giving Lett a little prod with his foot.

"He's not the one we're worried about," Fargo said. "Come in here and have a look at the cook."

"Careful, Doc," Muley said. "Don't step on the hand."

The doctor looked down, saw the hand clutching the skillet handle, and stepped over it. When he joined the men at the stool where the cook was sitting, he got a better look at Fargo.

"You sure do wind up in the middle of a lot of trouble around here," he said. "You got any whiskey?"

Fargo told him that if there was any whiskey in the shed, he didn't know about it.

Ransome shrugged. "Guess I can try to find it later." He examined the cook's arm. "Looks to me like you boys have done about all you could for him. If you can get him to my place, I'll put something on that arm and bandage it up, but it's not going to mortify on him, not the way you cauterized it. If he ain't all bled out, he's likely to make it."

"Can you get him to the doc's place?" Fargo asked Muley.

"If I get some help," Muley said. "Don't you think the doc should have a look at you? Your arm don't look much better than the cook's, except it's got a hand on it."

Fargo hadn't even thought about his arm, but now that Muley had mentioned it, it started to hurt. Pain throbbed through it all the way to the shoulder.

"It'll be fine," Fargo said. "I'll get the bandages changed later."

"And what about your friend there?" Muley asked with a nod toward Lett.

"I'll find somebody to see to him," Fargo said, thinking that business was really booming for Mr. Sloane.

The doctor was rummaging around the shed, looking for something to drink, but he didn't find anything.

"Goddamned teetotalers," he said, looking at the cook. "Gettin' to be too damned many of 'em to suit me. Well, I'll work on him anyway. Bring him along."

Muley called a friend from the tent, and they half carried, half dragged the cook out of the shed with the doctor leading the way. The cook's hand was still lying on the floor, gripping the skillet. Fargo didn't know what to do with it, but it was certain that the cook wouldn't be needing it.

Fargo had about decided to throw it in the stove when a dog came running into the shed. It stopped when it saw Fargo and started to turn around and leave. But then it saw the bloody hand. With a quick look at Fargo, the dog snapped up the hand. The skillet fell away, and the dog scuttled off with the hand in his mouth. Fargo didn't try to stop him. He figured that was as good a way to dispose of the hand as any.

Then Fargo realized how wet he was from the coffee that had spilled on him inside the tent. His shirt was soaked. He put his hand inside his shirt and brought out the drenched remnants of the map he'd spent all day drawing. It might have survived being wet, but the added strain of the fighting had just about destroyed it. It was soggy and torn, and the pencil marks that Fargo had so painstakingly made were blurred and in some cases obliterated. Unfolding it only made it worse.

Fargo looked at the remains of the map for a couple of seconds and then stuck them back into his shirt.

Going back inside the tent, he looked around. Only a few men were left, and they were talking among themselves.

"You all right, Mister?" one of them called out.

Fargo said he was fine. The loss of the map had hurt him worse than Lett had.

"What about the man who took that knife in his shoulder?" Fargo asked. "Is he all right?"

"Hell, that was Franklin," someone said. "He wasn't hurt too bad. Pulled out that damned knife."

"Yeah," another man said. "Let a week or two go by, and Franklin'll be tellin' folks he killed Lett Plunkett with his bare hands and took the knife off him after he was dead."

Everybody laughed in agreement, and Fargo said, "Can one of you men go let Mr. Sloane know he's got himself another customer out back?"

"I can," said the man who'd made the joke about Franklin. "What about the sheriff?"

"I'll talk to him," Fargo said. "It's time he and I got better acquainted."

"You don't want to get better acquainted with him, Mister. He's about as mean as Lett Plunkett. Well, as mean as Lett used to be before you kilt him. Best you let somebody else talk to him."

"No," Fargo said. "I'll do it. He's just the man I want to see right now."

"You're gettin' to be a real pestiferous fella, Fargo," Sheriff Olson said when Fargo explained what had happened. "First you come into town with a dead man tied on a horse. Then you're in Rose Malone's bathhouse when two more men are killed."

They were in the sheriff's office. Olson was sitting behind his desk, feet up, pretty much as he'd been the first time Fargo had visited him. He hadn't bothered to get up when Fargo came in this time, either.

"Henry killed those men," Fargo said. "They were trying to rob him."

"Maybe that's what happened, and maybe it's not. I don't think it is. But whatever happened there, you killed that man on the trail, and you're sure as hell the one who killed Lett Plunket today."

"Self-defense, Sheriff. There are eight or ten men who were there and saw the whole thing. And you could talk to that man who got Lett's knife in his shoulder. He'd tell you who started the fight."

"So you say. But that's still four dead men you've accounted for, no matter who started the fights and no matter who shot one of 'em. And you might not know this, Fargo, but Mr. Jonah Clark has filed a complaint against you on account of the way you beat up on two employees of his yesterday."

"Those employees of his threw Elias Shue out in the street, and I helped him up. That's all I did. They didn't take kindly to that, so they started a fight. Elias and I finished it."

"That might be your story, but that's not the way I heard it."

"I'm beginning to think you're calling me a liar," Fargo said.

"Nope. All I'm sayin' is that there's your version of what happened, and there's the other version. I could lock you up right now if I had a mind to and bring in a judge to sort things out."

Fargo knew Olson was telling the truth about locking him up, but he didn't think the sheriff was really going to do anything, much less bring in a judge. If he'd been planning to put Fargo in jail, he'd have done it already. Calling in a judge could present big problems for

Clark, unless the judge were bought and paid for in advance.

"You've let Clark run roughshod over everybody in this town," Fargo said, "jumping claims, among other things. A judge might think you're more guilty than I am. You're not enforcing the law. You're just taking the town's money."

Olson swung his feet off the desk and planted them on the floor.

"Mostly," he said, "I'm taking Clark's money. This job don't pay enough to keep a man in beer and whores, so I need a little extra. But how I run this town ain't any of your business, Fargo, because you ain't gonna be around much longer. If you don't leave here by tomorrow, I'll arrest you and lock you up. And we won't be needin' a judge because you won't get out of the cell till the last dog dies."

"I don't think you'd go that far," Fargo said. "And I'll tell you one other thing. If anybody goes after Elias Shue's claim, he's going to have to go through me to get there."

"I got a feeling that might be the general idea," Olson said, smiling. "That way the town won't be out the expense of feedin' you and providin' a bed for you. Now get out of here, Fargo. I got work to do."

Olson leaned back in his chair, swung his feet up on the desk, and tilted his hat down over his eyes. Fargo thought for a second about kicking the chair out from under him, but he decided against it. He didn't feel like getting into another fight right then.

Luman wasn't back in his room when Fargo went to the hotel to look for him, but the table and the chair were gone. Fargo thought that as long as Luman wasn't around, it might be a good time to pay a visit to the Lucky Lady. He wouldn't mind seeing Rose Malone again.

The saloon was crowded and noisy, but then Fargo thought it was probably crowded and noisy most of the time. Men in a mining town liked to have a good time.

Rose didn't seem to be around, but Bob, Rose's burly bouncer, was there.

And so was Luman. The two men had their heads together and seemed to be talking over something important. Fargo had thought Luman looked familiar when they'd met for the first time, and now he knew why. Luman had been in the Lucky Lady the night Fargo had arrived in town. He'd been at the faro table, bucking the tiger.

Nothing unusual in a man gambling in a saloon, Fargo thought, and nothing wrong with him being a friend of Rose's strong-arm man. But it was interesting.

Fargo started toward them, working his way through the men who were laughing, drinking, and feeling up the soiled doves. They wouldn't get too far with the feeling and squeezing, however, not unless they paid for it. Very little went for free in any saloon Fargo had ever seen, and he didn't think the Lucky Lady was any different.

Bob looked up and saw him coming in their direction. He said something to Luman, who nodded, and Bob then headed for Fargo. They met in the middle of the floor.

"Rose ain't here right now," Bob said. "And she wouldn't want to see you, anyway."

Fargo was beginning to wonder if anybody in all of Denver City liked him. Lett had tried to kill him, the sheriff had threatened to lock him up, and now Bob was warning him away from Rose. Come to think of it, Bob had been hostile toward him when they'd first encountered each other. Rose had implied he might be jealous, so his hostility was understandable.

"I believe you when you say she doesn't want to see me," Fargo said. "But I'd rather hear it from her."

He started to brush past Bob, but the bouncer took hold of Fargo's right arm. Fargo's face didn't give away the pain that he felt, so Bob smiled and put on a bit of additional pressure.

"You'd better leave, Fargo. Right now. Before you get into more trouble than you can handle."

Fargo took hold of Bob's hand. Bob tried to tighten his grip, but Fargo clamped down hard, as if he were going to crush Bob's hand into mush. Bob's face turned white, and he relaxed his grip. Fargo removed the hand from his arm.

He didn't let go, however. He continued to squeeze the hand as he talked.

"Rose might not want to see me," he said, "but that doesn't mean I'm leaving. I need to talk to your friend Luman over there for a while, and I want to do it in private. What I mean is, I don't want you to come around and bother me. Is that all right with you?"

Bob tried to say something, but only a kind of wheeze came out. So he nodded instead. Fargo dropped his hand and moved on through the crowd toward the table where Luman sat.

16

Luman didn't look happy to see Fargo, and he was a lot less happy when Fargo told him about the map.

"It might look better when it dries out," Fargo said, taking the map from inside his shirt and handing it to Luman.

Luman took the map between two fingers, holding it as gingerly as if it were a rattler while Fargo explained what had happened.

"This is no good to anybody," Luman said when Fargo had finished, laying the map down on the table. "It's no help at all. I don't see how we can pay you for this. Seth would never agree. After all, without that map, we don't have anything. No landmarks, no idea of the trail, nothing."

"That wasn't the deal I made with Rogers," Fargo said. "I mapped the route, which is what I said I'd do, and now I've mapped it again. I'm owed the money whether you do anything about your stage route or not."

"The way things are now, we can't go along with that. Someone has the original map, and within days, if not hours, they'll be working on a road to Leavenworth. There's no time for you to make another map, and that leaves me and Rogers out in the cold."

"Like I said, that's not my problem. I'm still owed my pay."

Luman didn't appear in the least concerned about Fargo's pay.

"I'll wire Seth again and tell him what the situation is

if you think it will help. But you can bet he won't authorize me to give you any money."

"I'll see you tomorrow," Fargo said. "I want my money then. You tell Rogers that I did the job I was hired to do."

"I'll tell him," Luman said. "I'll do my best for you." But he didn't appear to care one way or the other.

Fargo got up and went to the rough bar. He found a space between two boisterous miners, one of whom was trying to sing whatever song was being played on the out-of-tune piano. Fargo didn't know which was worse, the piano or the singing.

He asked the bartender for a glass of the low-grade whiskey, which was the only kind available there. He knew it would be awful, but he needed something to calm him down.

Fargo rolled a cigarette, twisting the ends so tight that he almost tore the paper. He struck a match on the bar and lit up. Then he took a drink of the whiskey.

It tasted as raw as Fargo had expected, as if it had been aged about two hours, and it roiled Fargo's stomach almost as much as his anger at Luman. But that didn't stop him from calling for another. He drank it more slowly than the first, smoking and thinking over everything that had happened since Red and Lett had opened fire on him, trying to get a handle on things and figure out some way to get his money. It seemed to Fargo that if Jonah Clark was behind everything, then he would be the one who had the map. And if Fargo could get it back from him, the situation would be resolved.

It wouldn't be easy to get to Clark, not with Toby and Barker looking out for him. If they had to face Fargo again, they wouldn't try using their fists on him. They knew better than that now. This time, they'd use their guns. And if that didn't work, Clark might have more men that Fargo didn't know about to send against him.

None of that bothered Fargo too much, however. What bothered him was the uncertainty. He didn't know if Clark had the map or if someone else had it. He still wasn't sure that Rose Malone wasn't mixed up in things somehow.

And then there was Bob. It was pretty clear that Bob didn't like Fargo, but had the bouncer warned Fargo away from Rose because she really didn't want to see him or just because Bob was jealous?

And what about Luman? Fargo wondered. Why did he seem so unconcerned about the whole mess? Maybe he was such a skunk that it wouldn't matter to him whether Fargo got paid or not, but shouldn't he be worried about the probable loss of the stage route, a route on which he and Rogers had hoped to make a lot of money?

None of it seemed to make sense to Fargo, but the second glass of whiskey and another cigarette calmed him considerably and allowed him to look at the good side of things, namely the two horses and saddles that he was going to sell to Carver at the livery stable. Even if he didn't get paid by Luman and Rogers, and he hadn't given up on that, not by a long sight, Fargo stood to make a profit on the deal.

Finally, there were Rose and Ruth to consider. If Fargo hadn't made the trip to Denver City for Rogers, he'd never have met them. Yes, he thought, there were considerable benefits to the job he'd done if he looked on the good side of things. But that didn't mean he didn't still have hopes to collect his fairly earned pay.

He finished his second whiskey and cigarette and left the saloon. He was on his way to the livery stable to pick up the Ovaro when he passed Clark's office and heard a ruckus similar to the one he'd heard the previous day, just before Elias had come sailing out the door.

The difference this time was that the argument was even louder, and that it was ended by gunfire.

Two shots exploded inside the building, and the sound reverberated up and down the street.

The shots were followed by a few seconds of silence, and then Jonah Clark stepped outside. He looked around at the crowd and said, "Someone go for the sheriff. Mitch Foley has been shot."

Since he was sending for the sheriff instead of the doctor, Fargo figured that Foley, whoever he was, wouldn't be needing any kind of medical attention.

And no one had to go for the sheriff. Olson, who must have heard the shots from his office, came ambling down the boardwalk, not seeming to be in any hurry. He might have been a man out on a Sunday stroll with his favorite lady friend, except for the wicked-looking shotgun that he carried easily in his right hand.

He stopped in front of Clark's place, and the two men had a short conversation in voices so low that Fargo couldn't make out any of it. When they'd finished talking things over, Olson turned to Fargo and the other men who were still standing around and said, "Seems like what happened here is that Mitch Foley got a little upset and drew his gun on Floy Barker. Now that was a purely stupid thing to do, since we all know Barker is about as fast with a gun as anybody in Denver City. Won't be any need to lock anybody up or have a trial, as it was a case of self-defense, pure and simple. Mr. Clark here is a witness to that fact. So there ain't no use for you to spend the day standin' around here gawkin'. I'll take care of things. That's what the sheriff's hired to do."

The little speech explained several things to Fargo, such as why there were no prisoners in Olson's jail and why the wanted posters hadn't been looked at. Olson's job involved mostly making sure that none of Clark's employees got arrested, no matter what they might have done.

There was a good bit of muttering among the men on the boardwalk at most of what Olson had to say, but he ignored it and went into Clark's office. It wasn't long before Toby and Barker emerged, carrying a man's body. Barker had the torso, and Toby had the legs. They looked comfortable doing it, as if it was something they'd done several times before. Olson followed them out and down the street toward Sloane's.

"Sons of bitches," said a man standing near Fargo, but

it was a whisper, and there was no chance that either Barker or Toby would hear.

"Yeah," said another man. "Old Mitch had hisself a good claim, good color ever' damn day, but Clark'll have it now. Wouldn't be surprised if he's already filed on it. If he ain't, he'll have done it before Mitch gets cold."

"Bastard'll have ever' claim that's worth a damn before this is all over." The man who was speaking seemed to notice Fargo for the first time. "You the fella that helped out Elias Shue yesterday, ain't you?"

Fargo nodded.

"Well, you better tell Elias to watch his ass, because Clark will sure as hell be after him harder than ever, now that he'll be addin' Foley's claim to his holdin's."

"Maybe I should just have a talk with Clark," Fargo said, moving toward the open door.

The man who had spoken to him put out a hand to stop him. "You don't want to do that, mister. Clark'd just as soon kill you the way he did Mitch."

Fargo pointed out that Clark didn't seem to like doing his own killing and that Barker and Toby were gone.

"Won't make no difference," the man said. "They'll catch up to you sooner or later. Back-shoot you, likely as not. That's the way they like to work it with somebody who can fight back. Old Mitch, he had sand, but he didn't know nothin' about guns. I'd be willin' to bet he never even drew on Barker. Barker just flat-out shot him down."

"He won't shoot me," Fargo said, "but thanks for the warning."

He brushed by the man and went past several others to get to the door. When he got inside the office, he could still smell the sharp tang of gun smoke and blood, but it didn't seem to be bothering Clark, who was sitting behind a desk going over some papers. Maybe he was getting ready to file for Foley's claim, Fargo thought.

Fargo didn't say anything, just stood inside the door, blocking the light from the street and waiting for Clark to acknowledge his presence.

Clark wasn't going to be rushed. He took his time, and

after a while raised his head to give Fargo an appraising look.

"Aren't you the fella who interfered in my business with Elias Shue yesterday?" he said.

"I wouldn't call what you were doing *business*," Fargo told him.

Clark clasped his hands together on top of the papers he'd been reading and leaned forward.

"Be that as it may, you did interfere. I don't like people who interfere with me, Fargo."

It didn't surprise Fargo that Clark knew his name. Men like Clark made it a point to find out about people who bothered them. And if he was the one who'd hired Red and Lett, it was possible that he'd known about Fargo for quite a while before he'd even been bothered. That was what Fargo intended to find out if he could.

"You're in the business of buying and selling gold claims, I believe," Fargo said.

Clark nodded and smiled. "Just a local businessman trying to make an honest dollar. Everybody knows that."

"Honest businessmen don't have people shot in their offices."

"If you were outside just now, you must not have heard what Sheriff Olson said. Nobody had Mitch Foley shot. He was causing trouble, and he drew his pistol on my associate, Mr. Barker. Barker couldn't allow that, so of course he had to defend himself."

"I can see how that might work," Fargo said. "Just good, honest business practice."

"True. And you can see how interfering with my business might not be healthy."

"It was Barker and Toby who didn't look healthy yesterday."

Clark frowned. "That was a blunder, but an understandable one. They didn't know who you were, and they underestimated you. They won't make that mistake again."

"You know who I am, though."

"Skye Fargo. Called by some the Trailsman. Been all

over. Fast with a gun and your fists. I know who you are, all right."

"But you didn't know yesterday, or you would have told your hired help not to mess with me unless they were ready to kill me."

"That's correct, Fargo. What difference does it make to you?"

Fargo thought it over for a second and decided to tell him.

"Two men tried to kill me along the trail the other day. And two more tried when I got to town. I had a notion that you were the one who sent them."

Clark sighed. "You see how it is, Fargo? That's what a bad reputation will do for you. Everybody thinks you're out to get them. However, as I told you, I'm just a businessman. Why on earth would I want you killed? You didn't mean anything to me two days ago." He gave Fargo a wolfish grin. "Not that you mean much more now."

Judging by everything that Fargo had heard about him, Clark was a man who would lie at the drop of a hat, just for the pleasure of it, without even thinking. But for some reason, Fargo got the impression that this time Clark was telling the truth. After having been so sure that Clark was the man behind the attempts on his life, Fargo was taken aback for a second or two by the realization that he might have been wrong about him.

Clark laughed. "If you're thinking I was the one trying to take your life, Fargo, you have another think coming. You weren't in my way before, and maybe you aren't now. Just walk wide of me from now on, and you'll be fine."

"You complained to Olson about me."

"Hell, yes, I did. What did you think? That I was going to let you beat up my men and not get warned off? If it happens again, I can have Olson lock you up in that little jail of his for a long damned time. But if you keep out of the way of me and my men, I'll let it go."

Clark talked like a man who thought he had a clear

advantage. If that was the case, Fargo thought, Clark didn't know as much about him as he thought he did.

"You and I don't have any quarrel, I guess," Fargo said. "Not about what I thought, anyway. So as long as you don't bother Elias Shue again, we'll get along just fine."

Clark laughed again. "You don't tell me what to do, Fargo. Nobody does, not about Elias Shue or anything else. Maybe you haven't noticed, but I pretty much do what I want to around here."

"No, you don't," Fargo said. "Not anymore."

Clark didn't seem bothered by Fargo's remark. He sat up and brushed at the sleeve of his frock coat as if to smooth out a nonexistent wrinkle.

"If that's what you think, Fargo," he said, "you're wrong."

"I don't think so," Fargo told him.

And then he turned and left the office.

17

Thinking over what he'd learned from Clark, Fargo forgot about getting the Ovaro from the livery stable and walked back to the Lucky Lady. He looked around for Luman but didn't see him. Bob didn't seem to be there, either, though it was possible he was hiding out somewhere on the premises, waiting for trouble to break out. Or waiting for Fargo to come back so he could warn him away from Rose again.

Fargo didn't think any trouble would break out at that time of the afternoon because there was hardly anyone in the saloon. A few gamblers played cards without much enthusiasm, and over in a corner a man was asleep with his head on the table, snoring loudly. His right hand was still curled around the bottle he'd been drinking from when he passed out, and his left arm dangled down beside him, his knuckles resting on the floor in a puddle of beer or something less pleasant. The bartender was polishing the bar glasses with a clean white towel.

A couple of the soiled doves were sitting at one of the tables, and they looked up hopefully when Fargo came through the batwing doors. When they saw who it was, however, they looked away quickly. Fargo thought that was an interesting reaction to his appearance, so he went over to talk to them. When he did, they looked at the floor, the tabletop, and the ceiling. Anywhere but at Fargo.

"You girls don't seem very friendly today," he said,

pushing up his hat. "I'd think you'd want the customers to have a good time."

Without looking directly at him, one of the women said, "We want you to have a good time. Just not with us."

"And why's that?"

The one who had spoken, a faded blonde with heavily powdered skin, said, "We saw you in here the other night, and we were told that we're not to trifle with you."

"That's not exactly an answer to my question," Fargo pointed out.

The other woman, a brunette with thin lips and a nose that was sharp enough to cut tin, said, "It's answer enough, mister. Why don't you go on and have a drink or play some cards with those other fellas. And leave us alone."

"Not until I find out if there's a good reason I should do something besides enjoy the pleasure of your company."

"All right," the blonde said with a shrug. "I'll give you one. Rose told us to keep our hands off you, and that's what we're doing. She don't want nobody to mess with you but her."

"Well, now," Fargo said, "that sounds pretty good to me, but I'm not sure it's right. Her friend Bob didn't seem to want me to see her."

"Bob." The blonde said it as if she might be cursing. "Bob would like to get in Rose's pants but he's got no more chance than a dog does of mountin' a horse. Rose don't sleep with the help."

Fargo said he'd been told about that.

"Yeah, but Bob don't give up so easy. He says one of these days he'll be so rich that she'll have to give him what he wants."

The brunette laughed. "As if that would ever happen. Bob'll never get rich. He'll leave Denver City like all the rest of us, busted or dead."

Fargo looked around the saloon again. Nobody had come in or left.

"Where is Bob, anyway?" he said. "I thought he was supposed to be around all the time."

"Not all the time," the brunette said. "He can go off for a rest now and then if he wants to, long as it's quiet the way it is now. Does it most every afternoon."

"What about Rose? I don't see her, either."

"She's generally up in her room when there's nothing going on down here. But if she comes out and sees us talking to you, she'll skin us alive and use our tits for tea bags. Why don't you go up and see her and get away from us?"

That sounded like a fine idea to Fargo, so he thanked the two women for their time and left them sitting there. He climbed the stairs and tapped lightly on the door of Rose's room.

"That better not be you, Bob," Rose said from inside.

"Farthest thing from it," Fargo said.

"Fargo? Is that you?"

"It is."

Almost as soon as he'd identified himself, Fargo heard footsteps inside the room, and then the door opened. Rose stood there giving him an angry glare.

"You have a lot of nerve," she said.

Then, seeing the puzzled look on Fargo's face, she took his arm and pulled him into the room, locking the door behind them. Fargo couldn't figure out what was going on or why Rose seemed to be mad at him.

"What's the trouble?" he said.

"You mean to tell me that you didn't come in my saloon an hour ago and ask Bob where the whore was, meaning me?"

Fargo said that he'd done no such thing. "And I never would," he added.

"That son of a bitch," Rose said. "That conniving son of a bitch."

"Bob?" Fargo said, knowing the answer already.

"Yes. He said you came in to have a drink downstairs and that when he went over to talk to you, friendly-like, he said you asked him for the whore."

Fargo grinned. "And I guess when I said that, Bob whaled the tar out of me and threw me out in the street to lick my wounds."

"Well, he didn't put it exactly like that," Rose said, and she laughed. "But that's close enough. And now you're going to tell me it didn't happen that way at all."

"It didn't, for a fact. I didn't even have a drink until after I'd talked to Bob. He told me that you didn't want to see me and that I'd better leave the saloon."

"That son of a bitch. And did you? Leave, I mean."

"No, I talked to somebody else, and then I had a couple of drinks. When I was ready to leave, I did."

"You should have come up to see what I had to say about it."

"Bob told me that you weren't here. I made the mistake of believing him, but now I see that I shouldn't have."

"You're damned right. I'll have to deal with Bob later. He's been working here for too long, and I can find somebody to take his place easy enough."

"So you're going to deal with him later?" Fargo said, smiling. "What did you have in mind for right now?"

"I think you can guess the answer to that question," Rose said. "Why don't you take off your clothes while I do the same?"

She didn't have to ask Fargo that question twice. He started to disrobe, and Rose disappeared behind her changing screen. When she emerged, she was as naked as she'd been the last time she'd stepped from behind it, and she walked over to Fargo and put her arms around him, pulling him tight against her.

Fargo's tent pole was erect, hard and hot as iron that had been in a forge for a couple of minutes, and it was pressed between his belly and Rose's, burning both of them.

"That feels good, Fargo," Rose said. "And it's all for me."

"If Bob doesn't come in and catch us," Fargo said.

"Most of the rooms on this floor don't have a lock on them," Rose said. "But mine does. We don't have to worry about Bob."

As she spoke she pressed her heavy breasts into him, letting him feel that her nipples were just as hard and as hot as his rod. Fargo thought that he might just spurt right then and there, but Rose pulled away before he reached the critical point. Taking his hand, she led him to the bed.

Lying down on her back, she said, "Do you like to look at women, Fargo?"

Fargo nodded, not trusting himself to speak just at the moment.

Rose smiled. "Have a good look, then."

Rose spread her legs slightly and began to run her hands over her ample breasts, caressing them and squeezing gently on the nipples. With each squeeze, she bit her lip as little waves of pleasure washed over her.

After a little of that, she reached up one hand and took hold of Fargo's rod and fondled it lightly with her fingers, with special attention to the sensitive tip. Her other hand made easy swirls on her stomach and then went lower, the fingers tangling in the fiery pubic hairs, then moving even lower to touch the tender lips of her vagina.

All that time she continued to manipulate Fargo with her other hand, and he was taking it all in. The sight of her pleasuring herself and him at the same time was so arousing that he thought he could feel his rod get even stiffer and longer than it was already.

Rose's breathing grew faster, and her fingers grew more industrious both on Fargo and on herself. For a second time Fargo was sure he was going to explode too early, but once again Rose stopped what she was doing just in time.

"Fargo?" she said, looking up at him from the bed.

Her right hand was resting between her legs, and her left encircled Fargo's tool.

"I'm right here," Fargo managed to say, though his voice was so husky it was more like a whisper than he'd intended.

"I want you inside me," Rose said. "All of you."

She moved her hands to her sides and spread her legs. Fargo eased himself on top of her and allowed the tip of his rod to touch her just at the opening of her nether lips.

She took him in hand and ran the head of his tool rapidly up and down the slick slit, moaning each time it touched her sensitive pleasure button.

"I can't wait, Fargo," she said, guiding him into her.

He held back deliberately, easing himself along a fraction of an inch at a time until she grasped him by the buttocks and forcefully pulled him all the way inside her. She held him there for an instant and then released him.

"Give it to me," she said, and Fargo did, no longer moving slowly but pulling out and driving back as fast as he could go.

Even at that, he had trouble keeping up with the frenzied motion of Rose's hips as she made sure to give both him and herself the utmost sensation.

It wasn't long before she started to quiver beneath him and then to shake as if seized with a chill and a fever, both at once, and she held him to her again as she went into spasm after spasm of release. As she did so, Fargo let go as well, streaming into her with one hot burst after another until both of them lay spent on the bed.

Fargo rolled to the side and rested until his breathing became regular again. Then he got up and rolled himself a smoke.

"Roll one for me," Rose said, sitting up in the bed, discreetly covering herself with the sheet.

Fargo rolled another cigarette and put it between Rose's lips, striking a lucifer to light both it and his own. They smoked in silence for a while, and then Rose said, "I don't suppose you'd be interested in taking over Bob's job after I get rid of the son of a bitch."

Fargo shook his head. "I'm afraid that's not in my line."

"I didn't think it was," Rose said, exhaling smoke. "You're not the kind ever to stay long in one place, no matter what the pay is. Or the extras."

She smiled when she said that, and Fargo had to grin as well.

"There are probably lots of women wishing you'd stayed with them a while longer than you did," Rose said then.

Fargo tried to look appropriately modest. "I wouldn't know about that."

Rose laughed. "Like hell you wouldn't."

Fargo pinched out his cigarette and started to get dressed.

"You don't have to leave so soon," Rose said.

"I have to get back to Elias Shue's claim. I promised I'd help him out for a while."

"Him, or his daughter?"

Fargo paused and looked at Rose. "You know her?"

"I've seen her. She's very pretty."

"No prettier than you," Fargo said, and resumed dressing. "I'm thinking Jonah Clark might try to steal their claim."

"And naturally you plan to stop him."

"If I can. But maybe he won't try." Fargo pulled on his boots.

"He's likely to. If he can't buy a good claim for a lot less than it's worth, he seems to manage to get his hands on it some other way."

"I know about that," Fargo said, cinching his gun belt around his waist. "He had a man named Mitch Foley killed this afternoon."

"Damn," Rose said. "Mitch was a good customer. If somebody doesn't stop Clark, there won't be anybody left to buy drinks or pay for my whores."

"Maybe Bob could stop him for you."

"Don't remind me of that bastard." Rose let the sheet slip away, exposing her breasts. Fargo could see the stiff nipples pointing in his direction. "You sure I can't persuade you to stay?"

Fargo shook his head. "I wish I could hang around, but I promised I'd get on back."

"Well, you know what you're missing."

Fargo shook his head and smiled ruefully. "I surely do," he said.

18

The days were long at that time of year, but Fargo had been in town for a while, and it was getting late in the afternoon, near about sundown, as he started back to Shue's claim. He rode slowly, thinking about all the things he'd heard that day. He'd added them all up, and he thought he'd pretty much figured out what was going on now. But even at that, he didn't have any way to prove whether his addition was right or wrong.

Either way, he figured it was time for him to be moving along. When he picked up the Ovaro, he made a final deal with Carver for the horses and saddles and told the livery owner that he'd be back in a day or so to collect. Fargo wasn't trying to get rich on the deal, so Carver was happy, no doubt thinking that he'd skinned the Trailsman.

Shue wouldn't be happy, however, when he heard that Fargo was planning to leave, but that couldn't be helped. Fargo didn't mind giving Shue a hand as long as there was other business to attend to in Denver City, but that business was about to come to an end, one way or the other. Fargo had warned Shue that he couldn't stay long.

Fargo planned to talk to Luman one more time and see about getting his pay. Considering what he thought he knew, he might even be able to collect, though he wasn't counting on it.

The little matter of Jonah Clark might also be settled before Fargo left the area. Fargo thought he might have pushed Clark far enough that afternoon to force his hand, but he'd have to wait and see about that. You never could tell which way a man like Clark would jump, and so far nobody had tried to bushwhack Fargo as he rode back to Cherry Creek.

But Fargo was alert to the possibility that someone might get the idea that it would be best to have the Trailsman out of the way, and when he heard a horse coming along behind him, he guided the Ovaro off the trail and into a stand of pines to wait for the rider to pass him by.

Fargo had his pistol ready, hammer cocked, when the rider got near, but even in the shadows of early evening, he could tell that the horseman was neither Toby nor Barker. He was, however, someone that Fargo recognized.

"Muley," Fargo called out.

Muley pulled back on his horse's reins and brought the animal to a stop.

"You can just go ahead and shoot me if you've a mind to," he said, putting his hands in the air. "I ain't gonna run and just get shot after me and my mount are all tuckered out."

Fargo rode out of the trees with his pistol trained on the base of Muley's spine.

"Why would I want to shoot you?" he said.

Muley lowered his hands, but he didn't turn around.

"Fargo?" he said. "Is that you?"

"It's me, Muley. Where are you headed at this time of the evening?"

"Tell the truth, I was lookin' for you. I went by the livery, and Carver said you'd left there not long ago."

Fargo kept his distance, and he kept his pistol at the ready. Muley had seemed all right after Fargo's fight with Lett, but Fargo didn't trust anybody on the basis of just one meeting.

"Why were you looking for me?" he asked.

"I thought I might give you a warnin'. That is, if you were of a mind to pay any heed to one."

Fargo relaxed a little. He lowered the hammer of the pistol and asked what kind of warning Muley planned to give him.

"I was back havin' a bite to eat a while ago," Muley said. "You might recall that I got interrupted the last time I tried it."

Fargo said he remembered and told Muley to get on with it.

"I got to tell it the way it happened," Muley said. "If I get in a rush about it, I might get it all mixed up."

"Go ahead then," Fargo told him, thinking that the warning must not be urgent if Muley was in no hurry about it.

"Well, like I said, I was havin' a bite to eat, when in walks Floy Barker and that Toby fella. They're the two hardcases that works for Jonah Clark, which I guess you know."

Fargo said that he knew, and Muley continued.

"Anyway, I wasn't tryin' to mess in their business. I know better'n to do that. Those two, either one of 'em would as soon slit your gizzle as look at you. But they was sittin' close to me, and they didn't seem to care much about whether I heard 'em or not. They don't think much of me at all, or anybody else for that matter."

Fargo wondered if Muley would ever get to the point, but he figured it wouldn't do any good to rush him. He'd already tried that, without success.

"One fella they don't think much of is you," Muley said. "They was talkin' about how they was gonna take care of you and Elias Shue, and they had plans for Shue's daughter, too, but their plans for her didn't involve killin', leastways not at first. That was gonna come later, after they'd had some fun with her."

Fargo wasn't surprised. Toby and Barker were about as worthless a pair as he'd ever encountered, and that included Red and Lett. The only thing that surprised him was the way Muley's voice rose when he talked about Barker and Toby's plans for Ruth Shue.

"I waited till they left," Muley went on, more calmly. "And then I sat there for a bit and thought things over. What I come up with was that you seemed like a pretty good sort of a fella, and Elias Shue is a kind of a friend of mine. And I sure wouldn't want them to do what they was talkin' about to that girl of his, either, the bastards. So what I decided was that I'd try to find you."

"So you went to the livery stable to look."

"No, sir. I sort of asked around a bit from some people I know, and one of them said he seen you ridin' off from the livery, so I went by there to see if I could find out whichaway you went. And then I come after you to give you a warnin'."

"I knew Toby and Barker would come after me sooner or later," Fargo said. "But I appreciate the warning just the same."

"Glad to do it," Muley said. "But I ain't given you all of it. You see, they said they was gonna do for you this very night."

Fargo thought it over, wondering if it could be a trap. He still wasn't sure he could trust Muley, but the story sounded likely. He'd been pretty sure that he'd pushed Clark to the point that he'd reveal himself, and he'd even hoped to provoke Clark into taking some kind of action, maybe send Barker and Toby after him. But he hadn't wanted Clark to send them after the Shues.

"What do you think I should do about all this?" he asked.

"If it was me, I'd let Elias know that he was in for a peck o' trouble, and then I'd light a shuck out of here," Muley said. "I wouldn't relish the thought of Toby and Barker bein' after me. But I ain't you, so I expect you'll do somethin' different."

It was apparent that Muley wasn't trying to lead Fargo into anything, and in fact he was advising him to make a run for it. So there was no trap.

Fargo holstered his pistol. "I'll be doing something different, all right. The question is, what are you going to do?"

"Well, I thought about that, you can bet. And if I was smart, I'd do zackly what I told you. I'd light a shuck out of here, get lost somewhere in the mountains, and stay there a while till things quieted down around here."

Fargo shifted in his saddle and considered Muley. It was too dark now for the Trailsman to make out the other man's face, but Fargo thought Muley's jaw had tightened just a little bit, giving him a look of mild determination.

"But you're not going to light a shuck, are you?" Fargo said.

"No, I ain't. I should, but I just can't turn my back on the Shues like that. 'Specially that girl. So if you're wantin' any help, I'll ride along with you." Muley paused and looked straight at Fargo in the gathering dark. "I gotta tell you one thing, though. I ain't much of a hand with a gun. I can shoot one, but I ain't sayin' how straight. And to tell you the truth, I've never throwed down on another man in my life. Comes to killin' one, I don't know that I got the guts for it."

"Maybe we won't have to find out," Fargo said.

"Yeah," Muley said. Even in the darkness Fargo could see a mournful look in the young man's eyes. "But then again, maybe we will."

Fargo had to laugh. "You'll do, Muley, you'll do. But we'd better stop jawing about things and get on down the trail if we want to help out the Shues. Toby and Barker might be there already."

"Could be," Muley said. "There's another way around, and they wouldn't want to be takin' this here trail where ever'body could see 'em."

Fargo kneed the Ovaro forward, and Muley rode alongside him. They hadn't gone more than twenty yards when Muley said, "I just thought of somethin' else."

"What's that?" Fargo asked.

"They said they's gonna bring Sheriff Olson along with 'em."

"Damn," Fargo said, remembering Olson's shotgun.

"Yeah," Muley said. "I thought zackly the same thing."

When they arrived at Shue's cabin, Fargo could smell the smoke from the cookstove, and everything seemed peaceful enough. He and Muley had taken care to arrive quietly, and they hadn't shown themselves until Fargo was sure that there were no other horses or riders

120

around. He was confident that if anyone besides Elias and Ruth had been there, he'd have known it.

"You go to the door and let them know we're here," he told Muley. "I'll see to the horses."

Muley didn't seem to mind being the one who got to go inside first. In fact, Fargo thought, he seemed downright happy about it. Fargo wondered if the young man didn't have a case for Ruth. He wouldn't blame him if he did. And it would be a relief to Fargo. He'd told Ruth that there was no chance that he'd be hanging around for long, but he'd feel better about things if she had Muley to think about.

After he'd taken care of the horses, Fargo went around to the front of the cabin. Elias was standing outside waiting for him.

"I thought I'd take a breath of air," Shue said. "Let those youngsters get a little better acquainted."

"They've taken a shine to each other, have they?" Fargo said.

"Seems likely. That Muley's a good boy, but I'm not so sure he's tough enough for this kind of a life. Might make a good storekeeper, though."

"If he had somebody to teach him a few things," Fargo said.

"And if he had him a start, like the kind I might be able to give him. I found some good color today, Fargo, and even a couple of nuggets. I think there might be a vein around here, maybe on my claim."

"No wonder Clark would like to have it for himself."

"He ain't got it yet."

"He's about to try," Fargo said, and he went on to tell Shue what he'd learned from Muley.

"Goddamn it," Shue said when Fargo was finished. "Seems like whenever a man is about to get a leg up, somebody comes along and wants to cut it off. Well, by God, it ain't gonna happen this time. Sons of bitches got my store back in Kansas, but nobody's gonna take my claim away. Which way you think they'll be comin' from?"

"Muley mentioned that the trail wasn't the only way to get here. What's the other route?"

"Let's go inside, and I'll show you."

They entered the cabin, where Muley and Ruth were talking in low voices. They looked up when the door opened and moved a little apart.

"Why don't you feed Muley and Fargo some bacon and beans if there's any left," Shue said to Ruth. "Maybe one of those biscuits you made, too. They're likely to need something sticking to their ribs before the night's over with."

Ruth said there was some food left, and she rustled up a couple of tin plates and filled them for Muley and Fargo, who ate while Shue explained their position.

He sat down at the table with them and drew on the top of it with his finger.

"Here's the cabin," he said, outlining a square, "and down here's the creek."

He made a crooked line with his finger and then drew in the trail that came out from town. Though the lines didn't actually appear on the table, they were easy enough for Fargo to picture in his head. He wasn't so sure about Muley, who couldn't seem to keep his eyes off Ruth, though he'd duck his head every time she glanced in his direction.

"Now about here," Shue said, putting his index finger at a point along the invisible trail, "you can branch off and come right along the creek. You'd have to go through a couple of claims to do that, but you could skirt around 'em if you were careful. There ain't too many claims that close to the town."

Muley was looking off at Ruth. Fargo poked him in the ribs, and Muley jumped as if he'd been shot. Fargo pretended not to notice. Ruth did, but she hid her smile.

Fargo said, "Is that the route you were telling me about, Muley?"

Muley was a little dazed, and he didn't quite seem to know what Fargo was talking about. Shue helped him out.

"That's one way. 'Course they could always loop around and come at us from this direction."

He drew it in on the tabletop. Fargo thought it over and said, "There'll be at least three of them. They might figure that if one of them came from each direction, it would give them an advantage."

"Might," Shue said. "If we didn't know they was on the way."

"But we do know," Fargo said.

Shue grinned. "Yeah, we do. We can spread out and look for 'em in all directions. And that's just too bad for those sons of bitches, ain't it."

"Unless we have it figured all wrong," Fargo said.

"Yeah," Muley said. "What if they all come from the same direction, and we're all spread out?"

"We'd be in a hell of a mess," Shue said.

"And what if they have more than three men?"

"Be in an even worse mess."

"Guess we'd better not be wrong about it, then," Muley said.

19

Even if they were right about what Clark's hired guns would do, there were still a couple of problems—Muley and Ruth.

Ruth insisted that she wanted to be involved in the fighting, and so did Muley, but Fargo wasn't sure that either one of them was capable of standing up to Olson, Toby, or Barker. And Shue didn't want his daughter to do anything more than stay in the cabin under cover.

But if they were going to cover all three approaches to the cabin, and if Clark's men cooperated and used those approaches, either Muley or Ruth was going to have to take a part. And if Olson or one of the others thought about coming at them from across the creek, or if they'd brought a fourth man, there was still going to be an unprotected side.

"I don't want Miss Ruth to get hurt," Muley said. "I can take up guarding one of those ways they might come at us, but she needs to stay here in the cabin."

"I'm not going to do that," Ruth said. She'd taken the plates off the table and was sitting at the table with the men. "I can do a lot more than just cook and clean."

"I know that," Elias said. "You're a big help to me with the claim. But this is different."

Fargo wasn't going to get into the argument. He didn't think it was his place to do so. However, they couldn't afford to sit around jawing all night, and he reminded them of that fact.

"We need to get into position pretty soon," he said. "They might not be here for a while, but we don't know for sure when they'll be coming."

"I got an idea," Muley said. "Ruth could stay here in the cabin in case anybody comes at us across the creek. We didn't think about that."

Fargo, of course, had thought about it, and he was glad that Muley had come to the right conclusion. It might not have been Muley's place to bring it up any more than it was Fargo's, but Shue accepted it.

"I think that's a good idea. Now let's get the rest of us settled."

Fargo took the position down the creek, with Shue up at the corral in back of the house in case someone looped around, and with Muley out toward the trail. Fargo just hoped that Muley could pull the trigger when the time came. The Trailsman didn't have any doubts about Shue, and none about Ruth, either. He thought she might be tougher than Muley.

Fargo was armed with his pistol and his rifle. Shue had a pistol, and so did Muley. Ruth had an old shotgun that Shue had kept for protection from animals but that didn't look any too trustworthy to Fargo. His advice to Ruth had been, "Don't shoot unless you have to."

Fargo was settled in behind a pine bole. He didn't expect anyone to be coming along for a while. The smart thing to do would be to wait until after the middle of the night, the time when everybody would be sleeping soundly, at least in the normal course of things.

The night was quiet for the most part, filled with the smell of the pines and the cool air from the mountains. Now and then an animal would stir somewhere, or a squirrel would move around in a tree. Fargo could hear the gentle rippling of the creek off to his right, and an occasional drift of breeze would rustle the pine needles. Fargo hoped that it wasn't so quiet where Muley was that the youngster would drift off to sleep.

Fargo was a little tired himself, what with his strenuous bout with Ruth the previous night and with Rose that afternoon, but he knew there was no chance he'd fall asleep. He was too aware of the danger they all faced from Clark's crew of toughs.

They came well after midnight. Fargo heard one man long before he got to the pine where Fargo was lying in wait. Whoever it was, he wasn't taking any care to keep quiet. He must have figured that there was nobody to hear him, which was a mistake he might not live to repeat.

Fargo planned to wait until he passed by the tree and then take him without causing any disturbance, but things didn't work out that way. The sound of a shot came from the direction of the cabin, and the man broke into a run.

There were more shots, and Fargo knew he couldn't waste any time. When the man ran past the tree, Fargo stuck out the barrel of his rifle. The man tripped over it and fell headlong to the ground. Fargo stood over him and slammed the rifle butt into the back of his head.

Fargo didn't bother to check to see who he'd hit, but when he bent down to pick up the man's weapon, he saw that it was a shotgun. So now Olson was out of the fight.

Holding his rifle in one hand and the shotgun in the other, Fargo ran toward the cabin, where still more shots were being fired.

Shots were coming from near the trail, too, where Muley would have been watching. It was beginning to sound like a small war had broken out, and Fargo supposed that's what it was.

He stopped just at the edge of the trees and looked toward the cabin. First he saw a bright muzzle flash from the corral, and then the shotgun boomed from inside the cabin.

Fargo couldn't see the targets, but he knew that Ruth would be shooting at someone nearby, maybe behind the woodpile that was about ten yards away. Fargo waited a second or two, and sure enough there was a muzzle flash from the woodpile.

The firing continued from the corral and the trail as

well, and Fargo had to decide what to do. There had been at least four men, not three, though Olson wasn't a factor any longer. Fargo needed to take another one out.

The man behind the woodpile fired again, and the shotgun responded. When it did, Fargo moved, running for the front of the cabin. When he was within its shadow, he leaned Olson's shotgun and his own rifle against the wall. He drew his pistol and slipped to the corner and took a look around.

The moon was a little past full and sliding down the sky toward the mountains, but there was enough light to give Fargo a good glimpse of the clearing beside the cabin, all the way down to the creek. He saw the woodpile clearly, a dark heap of cordwood stacked where it was just a short walk from the cabin.

After Fargo had been watching it for only a couple of seconds, a man's head rose above the wood, and Fargo snapped off a shot with his pistol. The man's head jerked back and disappeared. Fargo picked up the shotgun, went to the cabin door, and tapped on it.

"Ruth," he said. "It's Fargo."

He didn't have to wait long before the door opened, and Ruth stood before him.

"What happened?" she said. "What are you doing here?"

"I shot the man behind the woodpile." Fargo handed her the shotgun he'd taken from Olson. "This is a better weapon than the one you have. It's loaded."

Ruth took the Greener with her left hand. Her right still held the old shotgun she'd been using. She hefted Olson's gun and said, "Are you sure this one's better?"

Fargo said he didn't doubt it.

"You wait here," he added, "in case somebody gets past the rest of us. I'm going to see if I can do anything about the man who has Elias pinned down."

"What about Muley?"

They heard a shot from the trail.

"I don't know," Fargo said, "but he's still shooting, so he must be all right."

"I'm going to help him," Ruth said.

She shoved by Fargo and out the door, holding both shotguns. Fargo didn't try to stop her. He wasn't sure he could have. He thought about telling her to be careful, but he was pretty sure that wouldn't do any good, either. Women never took his advice. So he went around the house, sticking to the shadows until he came to the little corral.

It took a few seconds for him to spot Elias, who was lying beside the lean-to where the chickens would normally be roosting. He lay awfully still, and for a second, Fargo thought he might be dead. But then there was movement in the trees beyond the corral, and Elias fired a shot in that direction. Someone fired back, and Fargo took a shot at the place where the streak of flame had appeared.

"That you, Fargo?" Shue said without looking around.

"It's me. How many are out there."

"Just the one, I think. What about Ruth?"

"She's gone to help Muley. I didn't try to stop her."

"Might as well not. She's got a stubborn streak in her a mile wide. Comes from her mother's side of the family. You gonna help me get that claim-jumpin' bastard in the trees, or not?"

"I'll do what I can. Count to ten real slow and then start shooting. After you empty your pistol, don't shoot again."

"Why not?" Shue wanted to know.

"Because I'm going after that fella up there, and I don't want you to shoot me by accident, that's why. Now start counting."

"One," Shue said, but Fargo was already gone, running back around the cabin. He dropped his rifle near the door, turned the corner, and went past the woodpile toward the trees. He was nearly there when Shue started firing, one regularly spaced shot after another.

The man in the trees couldn't resist shooting back, and Fargo marked his location carefully before entering the trees where the man was hiding.

The Trailsman could move along as silently as any cat,

128

and he made no sound at all as he wound among the branches and limbs that would have pulled at the clothing or snatched the hat off someone less heedful.

When the smell of gun smoke became strong, Fargo stopped. His eyes had already adjusted themselves to the greater darkness among the trees, but he didn't plan to make any further moves until he was sure where his adversary was.

It didn't take him long to find out. He heard a low, muttering voice coming from behind a big pine tree and made his way toward it. Someone was talking to himself.

Fargo moved toward the tree. When he was about twenty yards away, he looked around until he found a sizeable stick on the ground. He picked it up and threw it hard at the tree.

The stick smacked into the pine's trunk and bounced off.

"Goddamn!" the man said and whirled around the trunk. It was Barker, and he started firing wildly.

"I'm over here, Barker," Fargo said.

The shooting stopped, and Barker froze. The moonlight that filtered through the tree branches mottled his face.

"I shoulda known you'd be mixed up in this, Fargo," he said.

"If you knew that, you should have stayed out of it."

"If I'd stayed out of it, I wouldn't have got the chance to kill you."

"You don't have a chance now, either," Fargo said, and as Barker raised his pistol and tried to trigger off a shot at the Trailsman, Fargo shot him in the chest.

Barker's shot went into the pine needles at his feet, causing some of them to bounce upward. Barker stared at Fargo and tried again to raise his pistol, but it seemed to have become too heavy for him to hold. It slipped from his fingers just as his knees buckled.

For a second after he went down, Barker appeared to be kneeling in prayer, though his eyes were still wide open and staring at Fargo. Barker opened his mouth, but it wasn't to pray, and no words came out. There was blood instead, and after a little of it had run down his chin, Barker fell over flat on his face.

Fargo left him there and started off toward the trail. When he was about halfway to the spot where he thought Muley would be, he heard a shotgun boom once. That sound was followed by a pistol shot, and the shotgun roared again.

After that, it was quiet.

20

"Well, we took care of 'em for good, that time," Elias said.

They were all back in the cabin. Barker was lying in the trees where Fargo had left him. Toby was behind the woodpile with the top of his head shot off. Fargo had left him where he fell, too. And a man that none of them knew was lying dead up near the trail.

"You shoulda seen the way Ruth took care of that sidewinder," Muley said. "Sneaked around behind him as smooth as any Apache. Near about cut him in two with that shotgun."

"We're lucky Olson didn't cut one of us in two with it," Elias said, giving his daughter a pat on the hand. "And it's a good thing Ruth learned to shoot one."

"Sure enough is," Muley said. "That sucker had me pinned down to where I couldn't hardly move."

"Muley's being modest," Ruth said. "He would have gotten him pretty soon if I hadn't been there to do it."

Fargo thought that just might be the truth. Muley had stood his ground and held the man off until Ruth arrived, which was almost more than Fargo had hoped for.

"I don't think Jonah Clark will be botherin' me any more," Elias said. "Much less tryin' to take my claim. Not when he finds out what he's up against."

Fargo wasn't so sure about that. Clark didn't strike him as being the kind who'd back off. He'd come after Shue again as soon as he could find somebody to carry a gun for him. Unless Fargo did something about it.

"What about Olson?" Ruth said. "I have his gun, but where is he?"

Fargo had momentarily forgotten about the sheriff. He said, "He's lying out there where I was waiting, with the back of his head bashed in."

"You right sure he's still there?" Elias said.

"I'd better go check. I hit him mighty hard, but he's probably still alive. And if he's alive, he's still dangerous."

"I'll go with you," Muley said.

Fargo could tell the young man was feeling his oats. And wanting to show off for Ruth.

"You stay here in case somebody else comes along," Fargo told him. "Olson won't be in any shape to cause me any trouble."

"You right sure about that?"

"I'm sure," Fargo said. "You can see about the bodies we've got scattered around here, maybe start getting them buried, and I'll see about Olson."

He took his rifle along with him and left them there.

When Fargo got back to the big pine tree where he'd been waiting, Olson was gone. Other than the obvious fact that someone had been scrabbling around in the pine needles, there was no sign that he'd ever been there.

I guess I didn't hit him as hard as I should have, Fargo thought. *Or it could be that he just has a damned hard head.*

Fargo looked around for a few minutes to be sure that Olson wasn't there and hiding behind a tree. All the Trailsman found was the place where the sheriff's horse had been tied. That made him think about the other horses. If Olson hadn't rounded them up, maybe Muley could sell them to Carver and get himself a start on a store without having to rely on Shue for it.

Fargo went back to the cabin and told them what he'd found, or hadn't found. Then he asked what they'd done with the bodies.

"Not a damn thing," Elias said. "They can wait till daylight. Maybe a bear will've carried 'em off by then."

Fargo didn't think so, but he didn't mind if Elias

wanted to wait. He suggested that Ruth and Muley look for the horses while he and Elias discussed what to do about Olson.

"I don't think I ought to take those horses," Muley said. "Don't seem right, somehow."

"Those men tried to kill us, Muley," Ruth told him. "They owe us something for that."

Elias agreed, and added that the horses might starve if they weren't brought in. "Or somebody else might find 'em and sell 'em. Now how would that sit with you?"

Muley saw that it wouldn't be right for that to happen, so he let himself be talked into looking for the horses. But he said he wouldn't try to sell them unless Fargo, Elias, and Ruth agreed to share the money with him.

"I won't be around when you divide it," Fargo said. "Besides, I've already sold Carver a couple of horses. You and Ruth can have my share."

After another short discussion, Muley was won over, and he and Ruth went out to see if they could locate the horses.

"That Muley's a better man than I thought he'd be," Elias told Fargo when Muley and Ruth had left the cabin. "I wouldn't mind havin' him for a son-in-law. But that's not gonna happen for a while. Right now we need to decide what we're gonna do about Olson."

"I thought that while those two are out looking for the horses, you and I could ride back to town and take care of him."

"I don't have a horse. Just that mule that pulls the wagon."

"Muley won't mind if you borrow his horse. He's going to have three of them if he can find them. Or would you rather stay here?"

Shue kicked the dirt floor. "I'm not tryin' to get out of it, goddamn it. I want to see that bastard get what he deserves, and Clark along with 'im. I just don't want to take the wagon. And I sure don't want to ride no mule, not that there'd be any shame in it."

"You won't have to ride the mule," Fargo said. "Load that pistol of yours and come on."

When they got into town, there was just a hint of false dawn in the sky, and the streets were deserted except for a big brindled dog that was trotting down the board-walk near Jonah Clark's office as if he had some impor-tant business to conduct there. When he saw the two riders, he ducked into an alley and disappeared.

"Where you reckon Olson went?" Shue asked. "Back to his office?"

Fargo didn't think so. "If I were him, I'd either have headed for the mountains or gone looking for Clark."

"Clark's got hisself a house," Shue said. "There ain't that many around here, but Clark thinks he's gonna own the whole town one of these days, so he's already started settin' himself up. Pretty nice house, too."

"Where is it?"

"I'll show you," Shue said, and nudged Muley's horse out into the lead.

They rode through Denver City, and Shue took a trail off in the direction of the creek.

"No claims on this part of the creek," he said. "No-body ever found any color here a-tall. So this is where Clark built his house."

The house was small but proper, with a yard enclosed by a white picket fence. There was even a flower bed.

"He's got hisself a Chinaman that takes care of it for him," Shue said. "He wouldn't stoop to dirtyin' his hands."

A light burned in one window of the house, and there was a horse tied to a hitching post beside the gate in the fence.

"Bound to be Olson's," Shue said, nodding at the horse. "What's our play?"

"We go in and tell Clark that it's time he left town and set himself up somewhere else."

"He won't like that. Won't do it, neither. He's got Olson to back him, too."

Fargo smiled. "And I've got you. Who do you think the odds favor?"

"Hell," Shue said. "When you put it that way, I can see we can't lose."

He slid off Muley's horse, and Fargo climbed down from the Ovaro. After they'd tied the horses to the fence, Fargo and Shue went through the gate and into Clark's yard along a swept dirt walkway. When they stopped at the front door of the house, Shue said, "We gonna knock?"

The light was in a back window, probably the kitchen, Fargo thought. For some reason people seemed to like to talk in the kitchen, even people like Clark, who most likely didn't do a lot of cooking.

"We'll see if there's a back door," he said. "Be quiet."

"You don't have to tell me to be quiet. A mouse ain't quiet compared to me."

They went silently around to the back of the house with Fargo leading the way. There was a door, all right, and Fargo didn't wait for Shue to catch up to him. He drew his pistol, raised his foot, and kicked in the door. It slammed into the wall and bounced back, hitting Fargo in the shoulder as he went through the opening.

Clark and Olson were sitting at a little table, both of them petrified with shock. Fargo leveled his pistol at them.

"Evening, gents," he said. "You can keep your seats. Mr. Shue and I just want to have a little talk with you."

Clark didn't move, but Olson did, going for the pistol he wore at his hip. He didn't even get it out of the holster before Fargo shot him in the right arm. He fell sideways out of the chair and onto the floor.

"He was faster with that gun before you hit him in the back of the head," Shue said, coming into the room. "Look at that, Fargo. You bloodied him up pretty good."

The back of Olson's head was indeed a mess of hair and blood, and now blood ran from his wounded arm onto the floor of the kitchen. Clark continued to sit, stony faced.

Fargo told Shue to help Olson up and back into the chair. It took a minute or so, but when the sheriff was seated again, Fargo said to Clark, "I told you that you weren't running things around here anymore, and I told Olson that if he tried to get to Shue, he'd have to go through me. Neither one of you listened. You should have."

Olson didn't have anything to say. He was in a daze, his eyes wandering, and he wobbled as if he might fall off the chair again. Shue put out a hand and steadied him.

"You have the gun," Clark said to Fargo. "So I'm listening now. What are you planning to do?"

"Nothing much," Fargo said. "I'm not the law, but then neither is Olson. There's a shortage of law around here right at the moment. So I'm going to let you leave town quietly. You can keep whatever claims you've stolen up till now because I don't want to try sorting that out. But you'd better not come back here again. If you do, maybe a citizens' committee will have the gumption to see that you get what you deserve."

Shue laughed. "You know, Fargo, I think I can just about guarantee that's what'll happen if he shows his face. If I wanted to, I could round up a few men right now that'd love to put a little tar and feathers on him and ride him out of Denver City on a rail."

"This is my home," Clark said, trying to maintain a semblance of dignity. "And I have a business to run here. I'm not leaving."

"It's not your home anymore," Fargo said. "And you don't have a business, either. Take Olson's horse and ride away from here right now."

Clark looked defiant for just a moment, but then Olson's eyes rolled up in his head, and·he fell off the chair again. Shue hadn't made a move to help him, and nobody seemed to care that he was lying on the floor.

Clark's shoulders slumped. "All right. I'll go."

He started to rise, but Fargo stopped him.

"Hold on," the Trailsman said. "You need to do something for me before you leave."

"What?" Clark said.

"Do you have ink and paper?"

"Of course."

"Good. Go get it. I'll go with you. Elias, you stay here and make sure Olson doesn't cause any trouble."

Shue toed Olson in the ribs, but the sheriff didn't move.

"He ain't gonna bother nobody," Elias said.

"Stay here anyway," Fargo told him. "Let's go, Clark."

Clark got up, and Fargo followed him into a room where there was a small writing desk. Clark lit a lamp that sat on a nearby table, and Fargo told him to have a seat.

"I want you to write out a deed to this house," he said.

He was going to tell Clark to make the deed in Muley's name, but it occurred to him that he didn't know Muley's real first name or his last one. So he just told Clark to make it in Elias's name.

"I'll be damned if I will," Clark said.

Fargo thumbed back the hammer of his Colt. "You'll be dead if you don't."

Clark got a piece of paper and a pen and started to write.

"Make it sound as legal as you can."

When Clark had finished writing, Fargo took the paper and waved it a time or two to let the air dry the ink. Then he read it over.

"Sounds all right to me," he said. He folded it and stuck it inside his shirt. "You can leave now."

"I'll need some things from the house. I should pack a bag."

"You don't have time for that. Elias might round up those men he was talking about before you got it done."

"At least let me take my shaving kit."

Fargo said Clark could do that much. Then, feeling generous, he added, "And get yourself a clean shirt, too."

Clark took some papers from the desk, with Fargo watching him all the time. Then he went to get the shirt and shaving kit. Fargo kept an eye on him.

"I'd ride for Kansas, if I were you," Fargo said after

Clark had gathered what he was going to take with him. "I hear there's always an opportunity there for a man like you."

"You can eat dirt, Fargo."

"I got a feeling you'll be doing that long before I will," Fargo said. "Now get along on your way."

"I'll have to stop at my office for some papers."

"You can do that. Just don't be there when I ride through."

Clark went outside, with Fargo following. The sun was coming up in the clear sky, touching the tops of the mountains. Clark mounted Olson's horse. He looked at the house and at Fargo one more time. Then he turned the horse's head and touched his heels to its side. He rode away slowly and didn't look back.

21

When Fargo went back inside the house, Elias had helped Olson to Clark's bedroom and put him on the bed.

"He was halfway able to walk in here," Shue said, "but he's passed out again. He ain't lost all that much blood from that bullet you put in him, so it must be that knock on the head that's causin' him the trouble. What you reckon we oughta do about it?"

"Get a doctor," Fargo said. "I know one, but I don't know where he keeps himself."

"This doctor you know, does he like a drink of whiskey?"

"That's the one. Name's Ransome. You know where to find him?"

"I can find him. You stay here with Olson, and I'll get him. Unless you want to just leave Olson here and let nature take its course."

"Get the doctor," Fargo said, and Shue left to do it.

While Elias was gone, Fargo sat in the kitchen and thought over what had happened that night. The way he figured it, Clark wouldn't be coming back. He could sell his gold claims in Kansas, or wherever he went, and set himself up in some other crooked business, which he'd probably choose to do rather than take a chance on coming back to Denver City. The loss of the house might anger him, but even the house wouldn't be worth the risk of coming back to face the men Elias might have waiting for him.

So that was one problem solved. Now all Fargo had to do was get paid for the job he'd been hired to do in the first place. He was mulling over the possibilities of doing that when Shue and the doctor showed up.

"Where's the patient?" Ransome said.

He was red-eyed from either drink, lack of sleep, or both, and he could have used a bath and a shave. But then he could have used a bath and a shave every time Fargo had seen him.

"In the bedroom."

The doctor didn't seem in any hurry for a man who'd been roused at daybreak. He set his bag on the table and looked around the kitchen.

"Isn't this Jonah Clark's place?"

"Used to be," Fargo said. "There's a hurt man in the bedroom that needs seeing to. Not Clark."

"Too bad. He could use some hurting." Ransome continued to look around the room. "Is he here? Clark, I mean."

"He's gone," Fargo said. "Left in kind of a hurry. Most likely won't be back."

Ransome was unconcerned. "That's fine with me. He ought to have left some prime whiskey around here somewhere if we could find it."

"You can look for it later," Fargo told him. "It's Sheriff Olson who's in the bedroom there."

"Olson?" Ransome rubbed a hand over his face. "How bad's he hurt?"

"We don't know," Fargo said. "That's why we got you."

"Far as I'm concerned, the son of a bitch can die. Be the best thing for everybody in town."

"He won't bother anybody again," Fargo said. "Even if he gets well. Now go take a look at him."

Ransome went, complaining about people who wouldn't let a man have a drink of decent whiskey. After a few minutes he came back into the kitchen.

"Just a little knock on the head and a flesh wound in his arm. I can take care of it pretty quick if you two want to get on out of here."

"We'll wait," Fargo said.

Ransome grumbled again, but he got his bag and took it into the bedroom.

"There's something I need to tell you about this house," Fargo told Shue when Ransome was gone. "It's yours now."

Shue just stared at him, so Fargo took the deed out of his shirt and handed it over. Shue held it out at arm's length and read it.

"I'll be damned," he said when he was finished. "That was mighty nice of Mr. Clark." He looked at the deed again. "He writes a fine hand. I don't suppose you even had to persuade him to write everything all out like that."

"No," Fargo said. "He thought of it himself. Said he wanted you to have the house. He thought you might give it to Muley. For a wedding present."

Shue looked at the document again, then folded it and set it on the table.

"Looks like Clark started out to jump my claim and got his own jumped," Shue said, laughing.

"I don't see what's so funny," Doc Ransome said, coming back into the kitchen.

"Ain't no use to explain it," Shue told him. "You wouldn't get the joke. How's Olson?"

"He'll be fine in a day or so. Is Clark going to let him stay here?"

"You can forget about Clark," Shue said. "This is my place now."

"Congratulations. You got any whiskey?"

"Let's look around and see," Shue said.

While Doc Ransome stayed in the kitchen to sample the bottle he'd found, Fargo and Shue talked outside near the fence. Fargo had thought he might stay in town, but Shue asked him to go back to the claim.

"Ruth and Muley'll need some help with buryin' those bodies, and they won't want you to get off without havin' said a proper farewell."

Fargo thought he'd prefer an improper farewell from

Ruth, but he knew he wasn't likely to get it now that she seemed to have set her cap for Muley.

"I'll stay here and look out for Olson, see that he gets sent on his way as soon as he's able to go. Ruth and Muley can work the claim until I get back."

"Muley might not want to," Fargo said.

"I expect he will. If he came back to town, he'd have to ride too far to see Ruth."

"All right," Fargo said. "I'll go back and tell them. And I'll see if they've got those bodies buried."

"If they don't, you could bring 'em in to Sloane."

"He's had enough business from me. No use in bringing him any more."

"Speakin' of business, we'll be needin' us a new sheriff here," Shue said. "If you'd stick around, I figger you could get the job easy enough."

"I appreciate the thought," Fargo said, "but I don't plan to settle down just yet." Fargo didn't bother to add that he didn't ever plan to settle down at all. "And even if I did, it wouldn't be to pin on a star."

Shue nodded his understanding. "Can't say as I blame you. Stop by here and say good-bye before you leave town if you get a chance."

"I'll surely do that," Fargo told him.

There were three horses in the little corral along with the mule when Fargo got back to the cabin. There was just barely enough room for the Ovaro.

Ruth and Muley were eating breakfast, so Fargo was invited to join them for bacon, eggs, and biscuits, along with a pot of hot coffee.

Muley told Fargo how he and Ruth had located the horses and brought them in.

"Wasn't time to do anything with the bodies of those dead fellas," he said. "We'd better get 'em in the ground right after we eat. Either that or take 'em to Sloane."

Fargo repeated what he'd told Shue about Sloane having gotten enough business lately.

"Then I guess we'd better get started with our diggin'," Muley said.

Fargo agreed, though what he really wanted to do was sleep. It seemed like he hadn't had any rest in a long time. If he didn't get some soon, his eyes were going to be as red as Doc Ransome's.

He knew he wasn't going to sleep for a while, however, so he drank an extra cup of coffee instead and went to help Muley with the bodies.

It was around noon when they finished. Fargo was hot and tired and dirty, and he told Muley that he was going to take a bath in the creek.

He stripped his clothing off out of sight of the house and went into the water. It was icy cold, and he could feel himself shrivel a couple of sizes as he sat down and plunged his head under.

When he pulled his head out and shook the water out of his hair, the air felt almost as cold as the water. Fargo was glad of it. The chill was waking him up.

He felt better when he'd gotten cleaner, but by the time he got back to the cabin, he was sleepy again. He told Ruth and Muley that he'd lie down under a tree and get some rest. They didn't seem to care. It was almost as if they had something in mind for themselves. Fargo smiled a little, thinking about it while he spread his blanket in the shade of a tree near the corral.

He didn't think about Ruth and Muley and what they might have planned for long, however, because almost as soon as he closed his eyes, he was asleep.

Fargo woke up just before sundown. The thin clouds were red and gold, and the mountaintops were blazing. Ruth and Muley were nowhere in sight, and Fargo wasn't about to go looking for them in the cabin. No telling what they might be up to. They'd have to do without bidding him a fond farewell, since he doubted he'd be coming back that way. But somehow he didn't think they'd mind.

He saddled the Ovaro and rode back to Denver City.

22

The streets were a lot busier than they had been that morning. Some of the miners were in town for an evening's entertainment, and some were there just for something to eat or for someone to talk to. As far as Fargo could tell, nobody had missed Clark and Olson, or Barker and Toby. Maybe nobody knew yet what had happened.

Elias would eventually tell someone all about it, Fargo was sure, but how close to the truth his account would be was anybody's guess. Fargo didn't really care. By the time word got around, he'd be long gone from Denver City.

Fargo left the Ovaro at the livery stable and walked to the bathhouse, where he found one bewhiskered miner bathing in the steamy atmosphere.

"Where's Henry?" Fargo asked the miner.

"Out gettin' some more hot water. You're welcome to the other tub if you want it."

"It has a patch on it," Fargo said. "It might leak. Anyway, I just want to have a word with Henry."

"Don't mind me, then," the miner said, leaning back in the tub and closing his eyes.

Fargo sat in the chair where he'd hung his saddlebags on his first visit to the bathhouse and waited for Henry to return. It didn't take long.

"Hey, Fargo," Henry said.

He was carrying a bucket and appeared to be wearing the same clothes he'd had on when Fargo first met him. Fargo wondered if he ever took advantage of the bathtubs.

"I'll be with you in a minute," Henry said.

He poured hot water from his bucket into the miner's tub and turned to the Trailsman.

"You lookin' to have yourself a bath?" he asked.

"I've already had one today. The water was colder than yours, but it was all right. I just wanted to ask you a couple of questions."

Henry looked at the miner, whose eyes were still closed. For all Fargo knew he'd fallen asleep.

"I don't know about any questions," Henry said, turning back to Fargo. "Rose don't like me neglectin' my duties here."

"It's your duties I want to talk about."

"I gotta get more water," Henry said, and went out the door.

Fargo got up and went after him into the storeroom where a bucket of water was heating on a stove. Henry set down the bucket he was carrying and started to reach for the one on the stove.

"You can wait and do that later," Fargo said.

"Better do it now. Don't want it to start boilin'. I might scald one of the customers."

Fargo put a hand on Henry's arm. "The customer can wait. You're going to talk to me whether you like it or not."

"The way you're lookin' at me, I damn well know I ain't gonna like it. Just let me set the bucket off the fire before you start blamin' me."

"I'm not blaming you for anything that happened," Fargo said while Henry moved the bucket. "You told me when I was here before that Rose liked for you to keep her informed about people who used the bathhouse. I just want to know who else you kept informed."

Henry rubbed his whiskers. "You know already, or you wouldn't be askin'."

"I just want to be sure. I don't like making mistakes. It was Bob, wasn't it?"

"All right, then, goddamn it. Yeah, it was. And I'm the one told Bob you was in here that night, but I didn't know there was gonna be any shootin'. I didn't even know who you were."

145

"But Bob did."

"Hell, I guess he must have. All I did was tell him what you looked like and how you was dressed. He seemed mighty surprised and made me tell him again. Then he told me to keep my mouth shut and went off somewhere."

Fargo knew where Bob had gone. He'd gone to find two men who wouldn't mind walking into the bathhouse and killing Fargo. In a mining town there were always a few men around who didn't mind a job like that, and Bob would be the one who knew where to find them. They were probably right there in the saloon.

"If I'd had any idea them two shooters was gonna come after you, I'd never have told him," Henry said. "And especially with Rose bein' there. If she'd got shot, I woulda felt awful."

"You'd have felt even worse if they'd shot you," Fargo said.

"That's the damn truth. Bullets was flying all over the place. I told Bob about it, you can bet. I told him to leave me out of his schemes from now on."

"And did you mention to Rose that you'd been spying for Bob?"

Henry looked at the floor. "Well, no, I reckon I might not've mentioned that to her. I didn't think it would be such a good idea. I guess you're gonna do it, though, ain't you?"

That was what Fargo had initially thought he'd do, but now that Henry had confirmed his suspicions, he didn't think he'd say anything to Rose about Henry's part in things. Fargo believed Henry when he said he didn't know what was going to happen. After all, he wouldn't have stayed in the room if he'd known there was going to be shooting.

"I'm not going to say anything to Rose," Fargo told Henry after he'd thought it over.

Henry looked surprised and a little bit skeptical. "You ain't? You right sure about that?"

Fargo said he was sure, and Henry thanked him.

"I really appreciate that, Fargo. I do. A fella like me,

there ain't many jobs he can get, and I'd sure hate to lose this one."

"If you do, it won't be my fault. I won't say anything to Rose, and don't you say anything to Bob."

"I damn sure won't. You got my word on that. But I thought you'd be havin' somethin' to say to Bob yourself."

"I will," Fargo said. "But not just yet. You go on about your business and keep quiet."

"You can just bet I will."

He started to thank Fargo again, but the Trailsman was already gone.

Fargo had hoped to catch Luman in his hotel room, but he ran into him just outside the bathhouse.

"On your way to the Lucky Lady?" Fargo said.

"I thought I might have a drink," said Luman, who seemed surprised to see Fargo. "And I thought you might have left town by now."

"Why would I leave? You haven't paid me what you owe me yet."

Luman didn't like hearing that. "There'll be no pay. You didn't deliver the goods."

"That's the point. I did deliver them. You're the one who lost them."

Miners were pushing past them on the boardwalk, and Luman tried to get away from Fargo. Fargo took hold of his arm.

"Don't be in such a hurry, Luman. We haven't finished talking."

Luman was getting nervous, and he looked edgy. "We can't talk here. There are too many people around."

"I know a place where it's nice and quiet," Fargo said, and he nudged Luman in the direction of the sheriff's office.

When they got there, Luman didn't want to go inside.

"I don't think Olson would appreciate it if we barged in on him," he said.

Fargo grinned. "Olson won't mind a bit. He's not here. He's not even the sheriff anymore."

Luman's eyes widened. "I didn't hear about that."

"Nobody else has, either. I'm not even sure Olson's heard it. But it's the truth all the same. You can take my word for it."

"I don't understand," Luman said.

"You don't have to," Fargo said, pushing open the unlocked door to the sheriff's office. "Go on in."

Luman went in, and Fargo followed him. It was dark, so the Trailsman went over to Olson's desk, took a match from his pocket, and lit the lamp.

Fargo set the chimney back on the lamp and told Luman to take a seat. Fargo sat on Olson's desk, picking up the keys to the cells as he did so.

Luman sat down. He appeared uncomfortable, as if he'd rather be somewhere else. Anywhere else. He looked at Fargo, who was rattling the cell keys in his hand.

"What's this all about, Fargo?" Luman said. "You know I can't pay you. Rogers has said so."

"I'm not so sure about that," Fargo said, putting the keys down on the desk. "But then there are a lot of things I'm not sure about. That's why you're about to clear them up for me."

"It all seems pretty clear to me." Luman twisted his hands nervously. "I don't know what you're talking about."

"You will," Fargo told him. "Let's start with that knot on your head."

Luman's hand went to the spot behind his ear where he'd been hit.

"Not much of a knot, is it?" Fargo said. "Already about gone."

"It was a lot bigger yesterday," Luman admitted.

"Not much bigger, though. I think that's because Bob didn't hit you very hard."

"He hit me hard enough," Luman said, and then his face fell as he realized he'd been tricked. "Goddamn it."

"I had it figured that way," Fargo said, picking up the keys again. "I just wanted to be sure."

He slid off the desk and walked over to Luman. Taking Luman's arm, he led him to the cells. Luman tried to pull away, but Fargo had a firm grip.

"For all I know, you'll be the first fella ever to spend any time in one of these," Fargo said, opening the door and shoving Luman inside.

Luman stumbled across the threshold, and Fargo closed the cell door with a clang. He locked it with one of the keys.

"You can't lock me up in here," Luman said, gripping the bars of the door. "You're not the sheriff."

"No, but I have the keys. Maybe if you give me the right answers to some questions, I'll let you out. If you don't, you'll have to stay here till somebody finds you."

"The sheriff will find me."

"Not likely. He won't be coming back."

Luman turned his head and looked at the cell. A cot ran along the back wall, and there was a chamber pot on the floor beneath it. That was the extent of the furnishings. Luman looked back at Fargo.

"Ask your questions," Luman said.

"I think I know most of what went on. I just want to be sure I've got it right. You and Bob must have planned it all together. I can't quite figure out why you wanted to steal the map, since I was bringing it to you. All you had to do was wait for me."

Luman sagged against the bars. "It wasn't me. It was Bob. At least at first. I was around the saloon too often, I think, and I was gambling too much. And losing. I probably talked too much besides. I mentioned the stage line that Rogers and I were going to start up. Bob seemed interested, and he wanted to know all about the plans we had."

"Bob needed money," Fargo said. "He had some plans of his own."

"I don't know about that."

Fargo knew, but he didn't see any need to get into a discussion of it with Luman.

"I just know that Bob asked me who was mapping the route," Luman said, "and about where it was going to be. I didn't know what to tell him about that, not exactly, but I did mention the general vicinity. And I told him about you, not that I knew very much."

Bob wouldn't have had any trouble finding out a lot more, Fargo thought. There was plenty of talk out there about the Trailsman.

"I should have figured it out from the very beginning," Fargo said. "You and Rogers were the only ones who knew I was on the way here and roughly what route I'd be taking. So one of you had to have told those hired killers where to find me along the way. It couldn't have been Rogers. He's the one who hired me. So it had to be you."

"I didn't tell those men where you were. Bob did."

"You're the one who told Bob, though."

"That's true, but I had no idea he was planning to have you killed and steal the map," Luman said. "He didn't tell me anything about that. And then you turned up in town very much alive. He knew then that his hired guns had failed him."

"So he just got him a couple more."

"I suppose men like that aren't hard to find in a mining town."

"They're not. But he should have found some better ones."

"Yes. He wasn't expecting you to survive again, even though he'd heard that you weren't easy to kill. Anyway, after you disposed of those two, Bob came to me. He knew that I'd been gambling too heavily, and losing. He said that he could take care of my gambling debts if I'd give him the map when you delivered it."

"But you couldn't just hand it over. You could never have explained that."

"No," Luman said. "And I didn't want to do it at all, but I needed the money quickly. Some of the men I owed it to aren't the forgiving kind. So we came up with the idea that we'd stage a robbery. Bob would hit me just hard enough to make things look right, and he'd take the map."

"And now Bob has it."

"That's right."

"And you have the money Rogers was going to pay me, but you decided to keep it for yourself."

Luman let go of the bars and walked to the cot. It took him only a couple of steps. When he turned back to Fargo, he looked like a man who'd just taken a beating.

"I told you I needed money. Bob took the maps, but he didn't pay me. He just laughed when I insisted. So I had to use your money to pay my gambling debts."

"So you've already paid them?"

Luman sagged down onto the cot. "Yes. I don't have your money. And I don't think you'll be getting it from the men I gave it to."

"If you were never planning to pay me, why in hell did you ask me to redraw the map?"

"It was just a way to stall you because you wouldn't go ahead and leave town. If you hadn't ruined it yourself, I'd have done something to it. I'd have told you that Rogers wasn't going to pay."

"And what if I'd gone to Rogers?"

"I'd have left town by then. Started over somewhere."

Luman might have been fooling himself, but he wasn't fooling Fargo even a little bit. Luman wouldn't have gone anywhere. He'd have stayed there in Denver City, probably trying to win back the money he'd lost and going deeper in the hole every night until somebody finally took him into an alley and put him out of his misery. He was better off being locked up in the jail.

"What are you going to do, Fargo?" Luman asked. "I don't have your money, and there's no way you can get it back."

"Has Bob found anybody to throw in with him on setting up his stage line?"

"He was going to talk to Jonah Clark about it. That's all I know."

"Then he hasn't found anybody. So here's what we're going to do, Luman."

"We?"

"That's right. Now listen."

Luman did, and Fargo told him his plan.

151

23

The plan would have been fine, Fargo thought later, if it had only worked.

It was simple enough. Fargo would let Luman out of the cell, and Luman would go to the Lucky Lady, where he'd find some way to get Bob outside. Fargo would take over after that, and Bob would be in the cell that Luman had occupied. That way, Fargo thought, he'd be able to get the map back. And then he'd give it to Luman.

The plan was good for Luman, because with the map back in his hands, he could tell Rogers that they were in business again. They could start the stage line as planned, and Luman would be off the hook for what he'd done to Fargo. And, just maybe, Rogers would be willing to pay Fargo all or part of his fee for having recovered the map.

Luman seemed to think it was a fine idea, and he'd played along with Fargo from the start. It was only after he went into the saloon that he had a change of heart, not to mention a change of direction, because after fifteen minutes, he still hadn't come back out with Bob.

Fargo gave Luman another couple of minutes. When he still hadn't come out of the Lucky Lady, Fargo pushed through the batwing doors and went inside.

The saloon was noisy, crowded with unwashed miners having a good time. Some were dancing, some were gambling, and all of them were drinking. There was no sign of Luman.

Bob was there, however, leaning against a wall and

tapping the toe of his right boot in time with the piano while he watched the crowd to make sure there wasn't any trouble.

Fargo admired Bob's ability to keep time with the piano, which seemed to be even more out of tune than it had been the last time Fargo had heard it. The song sounded something like "Camptown Races," and maybe that's what it was. Fargo couldn't be certain. He shoved through the dancers and made his way over to where Bob stood.

"If you're looking for Rose, she's not here," Bob said, raising his voice so he could be heard.

"And she doesn't want to see me," Fargo said.

"That's right, Fargo. Maybe you're not as stupid as you look."

"Maybe not. Have you seen Luman lately?"

Bob pushed himself away from the wall.

"Yeah. I saw him. He passed through on his way out the back door. Why?"

"I wanted to talk to him," Fargo said, thinking that he'd underestimated what a skunk Luman was. Instead of helping Fargo out and taking a chance of getting back on track with Rogers, he'd ducked out and left it all up to Fargo. Maybe he hadn't trusted the Trailsman, being such a treacherous sort himself.

"Why don't you go look for him," Bob said. "Rose doesn't want you hanging around here anymore."

Fargo was getting tired of Bob's lies about Rose. "That's not what Rose told me."

Bob gave Fargo a slow smile. "You calling me a liar, Fargo?"

"I guess you could say that."

"Then why don't you do something about it?"

That was exactly what Fargo intended, but he didn't want to start anything in the saloon. It was too crowded, and you never knew what might happen in a crowd. He needed to get Bob outside, closer to the jail.

"Why don't we go where we can talk without yelling at each other," Fargo said.

It was another one of those good ideas that would

have worked out just fine if Bob had cooperated. But he didn't. Instead he swung a big fist around at the side of Fargo's head.

Fargo saw the blow coming and managed to duck under most of it. Bob's fist grazed the top of Fargo's hat, knocking it off.

In dodging, Fargo bumped into one of the dancing miners, who stopped his high stepping and pushed Fargo away. Fargo collided with a table, and poker chips and money went flying. One of the gamblers was upended and accidentally kicked a man at the next table.

The man who got kicked didn't know what had happened or who had started things, but he knew he didn't like what had happened to him. He jumped up and pulled a knife from his boot.

Someone hit him before he could use the knife, and he fell to the floor, the knife dropping from his limp fingers.

And then confusion took over in the Lucky Lady. It seemed as if everyone was fighting someone. There was so much shouting and turmoil that Fargo couldn't even hear the piano, which he figured was no great loss, and for just a second he lost sight of Bob.

The next thing Fargo knew, something hit him in the middle of the back, knocking him forward across one of the poker tables, which hit the wall and collapsed beneath him.

Before Fargo could move, Bob landed right in the middle of his back with both bony knees. It was almost like being stabbed. The breath went out of Fargo all at once, and he nearly lost consciousness from the pain. Bob might have finished him then if someone hadn't hit the bouncer across the back with a chair. He fell off Fargo, who rolled to the side and reached for his pistol.

The pistol was gone, having fallen from the holster in the fray. Fargo knew he wasn't going to be able to find it in time to use it on Bob, so he grabbed hold of a nearby miner and pulled himself to his feet.

"What the hell?" the miner said.

He would have said more, but he didn't get a chance.

His legs were cut from under him by a kick from another man, and both of them went down. Fargo would have gone down as well if he hadn't already let go of the miner.

Fargo struggled to get his breath, and his back felt as if he'd been branded. He looked around for Bob and saw the burly bouncer crawling along the wall, avoiding kicking feet and falling bodies. He even avoided a whiskey glass that someone threw at him. It bounced off the wall and fell behind him.

Fargo started in Bob's direction, and his foot kicked something solid. Looking down, Fargo saw his pistol. He picked it up, but Bob had disappeared again.

Rose, however, had shown up. She stood on the balcony, looking down on the brawl with grave disapproval. Fargo couldn't blame her. There was going to be a lot of damage, and it would be a while before people started drinking again.

Rose caught Fargo's eye. All he could do was shrug, and then he was shouldering his way through the mob to get to the back door before Bob did.

But he was too late.

When he stepped out the door, Fargo took a shallow breath of the cool evening air. He couldn't breathe as deeply as he wanted to because he still hadn't recovered from being kneed in the back, and each breath burned him.

It was much quieter in the alley than it had been in the Lucky Lady, for which Fargo was grateful, though he could still hear some of the noise from inside. He looked around for Bob but didn't see him, and he had no idea which direction might be the right way to go.

He didn't have to wonder for long. A gunshot cracked the night, and a bullet smacked into the rain barrel beside Fargo, puncturing the side. Water spurted out onto the dust of the alley.

Fargo crouched down beside the barrel and waited. No more shots came, and he stood up and ran toward the end of the alley. When he reached the corner, he saw Bob running along the boardwalk in the direction of Jonah Clark's office.

Maybe he thought that Clark would be there to help him, or maybe he was just looking for a place to hide. It didn't matter to Fargo. He followed along at a shuffle-trot, struggling a little to get air into his lungs.

The people on the street paid no attention to what was going on. Either they hadn't heard the gunshot, or they didn't want to have to take sides. Or maybe gunshots weren't uncommon in Denver City. Certainly no one seemed concerned.

Bob stopped in front of Clark's office and tried the door. It was locked, so he went on, turning down the alley beside the building. Fargo wasn't far behind now, but he didn't relish the idea of going into the alley after Bob. The moon gave some light, but not enough to dispel all the shadows between the buildings. Bob could be hiding anywhere.

But Bob had the map, or knew where it was, and Fargo wanted it.

So he went into the alley. He was careful, taking a quick look first. Seeing no one and nothing, he slipped along the wall, sticking to the shadows. No rain barrel sat in this alley, but a pile of junk lumber lay at the back, scraps left over from construction of the buildings along the boardwalk. There was nowhere Bob could be except behind the lumber, Fargo thought, unless he'd gone over the fence or headed down the back alley to the left or the right.

Fargo thought he'd have heard anybody of Bob's size trying to get over the fence, so that left the lumber pile or the alley. Fargo was betting on the lumber, and he approached it by gliding along the wall of the building.

He stopped when he reached the corner. If he was wrong about Bob being behind the lumber, he was going to be in trouble. If Bob was standing at either side of the alley, he'd be able to take a clear shot at Fargo when the Trailsman showed himself.

While he was trying to decide what to do, Fargo heard a dog snarl behind Clark's office. The snarling grew louder, and something thumped against the back of the building.

"Goddamn!" Bob said.

Well, thought Fargo, *now I know where he is.*

There was another thump, and Fargo turned the corner to see Bob, who was about to put a bullet into the brain of a big brindled dog. It was the same dog that Fargo had seen the previous night, and it had its teeth sunk into the leg of Bob's pants. It was shaking its head from side to side, thumping Bob into the building and making it hard for Bob to get off a shot without hitting his own shin or foot.

"Don't shoot the dog, Bob," said Fargo, who didn't blame the dog a bit for not liking him.

Bob looked around at Fargo and said, "All right, then, I'll just shoot you."

But Fargo shot Bob first.

Bob dropped his pistol and fell back against the wall. He slid down it to sit in the alley, leaving a dark stain behind.

The dog, frightened by the noise of the shot, let go of Bob's pants and scooted under the building, out of sight. When Fargo reached Bob, he could hear the occasional squeal of a small puppy.

"She was just taking care of her kids," Fargo said, looking down at Bob, who was leaning back against the building while holding his right shoulder. Blood seeped out between his fingers.

"I hope you don't have that map in your shirt pocket," Fargo said, kicking Bob's pistol farther down the alley. "It would seriously piss me off if you got blood on it."

"You can go to hell, Fargo."

"I think I'll see if I can call up that dog," Fargo said. "Let her take a big bite out of you this time. Or maybe I'll just let you bleed to death."

"You better get a doctor if you want that map. I can't tell you where it is if I'm dead."

"I know a good doctor, all right," Fargo said. "He'll fix you right up for the price of a drink. But I want the map first."

"I don't have any map."

Fargo reached down and tapped Bob's wounded shoulder with his pistol barrel.

"Jesus!" Bob said. "That hurts."

"Not near as bad as it will if I set that dog on you."

"I'll give you the goddamn map, then. It's in a wallet inside my shirt."

Bob started to reach for it, but Fargo stopped him.

"I'll get it," the Trailsman said. "I don't want your bloody fingers on it."

He unbuttoned the shirt with his left hand, keeping his pistol trained on Bob's head. When he had the wallet in his hand, he backed away and opened it. Sure enough, the map was there.

"All I wanted was to make some money," Bob said. "So Rose would like me."

"She liked you well enough to hire you," Fargo said. "You should have been satisfied. That was as good as it was ever going to get."

"To hell with that. What about the doctor?"

"Stand up," Fargo said. "We'll see if we can find him."

24

Fargo sat in Rose's room. He was in the chair, and she sat on the edge of her bed. Both were fully dressed, and Rose's face was set in a serious frown.

"You nearly put me out of business tonight," she said.

"Wasn't me who did that," Fargo said. "It was Bob."

"And that's another thing. Now that you've put Bob in jail, just what am I supposed to do to keep order around here?"

"Bob wouldn't be much good to you anyway, not till that arm heals up," Fargo said. "And I think you said you could find someone else easily enough."

"You talk as if you thought I was the one at fault here."

"Well," Fargo said, "you were the one who wouldn't let Bob get close to you. He thought if he could earn enough money, he could impress you and get in your bed."

"Do you think I'd have let him, no matter how much money he had?"

Fargo wasn't sure, but he knew the right thing to say. "No. Not somebody like that."

"You're damned right. I only sleep with people I like." She gave Fargo a hard look. "And sometimes I make a mistake about that."

Her attitude didn't bother Fargo. "You don't really think I was a mistake do you?"

Rose had to laugh. "No, Fargo. I don't. You're one of a kind, and I'm proud to have made your acquaintance."

Fargo had told Rose pretty much the whole story, omitting only his dalliance with Ruth. She was glad he'd gotten the map back and amazed that he'd let Jonah Clark off so lightly.

Fargo didn't think it was light at all. It wasn't his job to enforce the law, and Clark had lost his house and business. He might have the claims, but he still had to find someone to sell them to. He certainly couldn't work them all himself, and it wasn't too likely that he'd find enough men to work them for him. Some of the men who had originally owned them would probably be able to get them back now that Clark was gone. That seemed like justice enough to Fargo. As for Luman, Fargo figured he'd wind up drunk and shot for his gambling debts within a year.

"I don't suppose you'd like a job working here at the Lucky Lady," Rose said. "You could do it better than Bob, and that's for sure."

"I don't like inside work. And the idea of a regular job? I don't like that much, either. I'll be leaving tomorrow, after I send a telegram to Rogers and get his answer. And I have to stop by and say so long to Elias Shue."

"I could try persuading you to stay and take that job I offered you."

"I'd like that a lot," Fargo said. "But it wouldn't work. I'd just leave anyway."

Rose got up and went over to the changing screen. She put one hand on top of it and looked over her shoulder at Fargo.

"Even if you're not going to stay, I could try to persuade you, couldn't I? Or do you think that would be a waste of time?"

Fargo smiled. There was one thing he knew for sure, and that was Rose's methods of persuasion wouldn't be a waste of time.

"You go right ahead and try," he said. "To tell you the truth, I'm looking forward to it."

"To tell you the truth," Rose said, stepping behind the screen, "so am I."

LOOKING FORWARD!
The following is the opening
section from the next novel in the exciting
Trailsman series from Signet:

THE TRAILSMAN #284

DAKOTA PRAIRIE PIRATES

Dakota Territory, 1861—where blood was thicker than water, and greed was thicker than both.

The two roustabouts were going to cause trouble.

They swaggered across the hurricane deck of the *Northern Lights,* bumping into passengers and glaring at anyone who dared comment about their drunken state. The big one was called Finn, his stocky companion was known as Slick, and they were the worst sort of river rats. The kind who would rather loaf than work. The kind who drank on the job, and the captain be damned. The kind who delighted in bullying others.

Skye Fargo saw them come up the main stairway. He stood near one of the *Northern Lights'* smokestacks, unnoticed in the shadows. A big man in his own right, he wore buckskins, a red bandanna, and a dusty white hat with the brim pulled low over his lake-blue eyes.

Strapped to his waist was a Colt that had seen a lot of use.

Finn and Slick were almost to the jack staff and the woman standing beside it. Amanda Stain did not notice them, or if she did, she did not let on. A stunning brunette, she was dressed in the height of fashion in a dress that clung to her shapely figure as if painted on. Her hat fluttered slightly in the breeze, and she held a parasol across one shoulder to ward off the worst of the burning sun.

Fargo was in motion before Finn and Slick stopped. He saw them halt and openly ogle Amanda, saw Finn nudge Slick and grin and walk up to her and say something. It caused her to stiffen but she did not reply. By then Fargo was close enough to overhear.

"I'm talking to you, bitch, and you'd damned well better mind your manners or else."

Amanda turned from the rail and regarded him coldly. "How strange that you of all people should be concerned about proper behavior, Mr. Finn. You are a lout and a lecher, and if you had a shred of decency in your uncouth body, you would not impose yourself on a lady."

Slick snickered and said, "Why, Finn, I don't think she likes you much!"

The roustabout did not like being mocked any more than he liked being insulted. "You and your airs!" He gripped Amanda's right arm. "You've been looking down your nose at me this whole trip, you and those snotty kin of yours. I have half a mind to slap you silly."

Amanda did not try to break free. She calmly met his lewd gaze and responded, "Persist in this behavior and I will have no choice but to report you to Captain Bettles."

Finn and Slick both laughed, and Slick slapped his thigh and declared, "Go right ahead! For all the good it will do you."

"Our weak-kneed captain doesn't have enough sand to fill a thimble," Finn told her. "We can do whatever we want and get away with it." He leaned closer. "Including having our way with any skirt we take a fancy to."

"Release me this instant," Amanda said.

"And what if I don't?" Finn challenged her.

By then Fargo was there. He did not tap Finn on the shoulder and politely ask the two roustabouts to behave. He did not say anything at all. He simply grabbed Finn by the shoulder, spun him around, and drove his knee into Finn's groin.

Finn doubled over and clutched himself. Staggering against the rail, he turned beet red and tried to say something, but all he could do was sputter.

"What the hell?" Slick blurted, rousing to life and clawing for a dagger he wore in a leather sheath on his left hip. "No one does that to my friend!"

Fargo had his Colt out before the weasel could blink and slammed the barrel across Slick's temple not once but twice, and on the second blow, Slick's knees buckled, and he oozed to the deck with spittle dribbling down his chin. Twirling the Colt back into his holster, Fargo turned to the lovely woman they had been abusing. "I can escort you to your cabin if you want."

"Whatever for?" Amanda Stain asked. "You have the situation well in hand, Mr. Fargo. Although I wonder if it was necessary to be quite so violent."

Fargo nudged Slick's unconscious form. "Violence is all men like him ever understand."

"Know that for a fact, do you?" Amanda asked. "Politeness can go a long way if you give it a try."

"It wasn't doing you a damn bit of good, was it?" Another minute and they would have ripped off your dress."

Amanda laughed and twirled her parasol. "Honestly, now. In broad daylight? With all these people around?"

Fargo sighed and regarded the other passengers, most of whom had frozen with shock and were standing well back. "These sheep? Finn doesn't care about them. He takes what he wants when he wants it, and he wanted you."

"I still say you overreacted," Amanda insisted, but then her voice softened and she said, "Nonetheless, I thank you for coming to my rescue. Sir Galahad in buckskins. Who would have thought there was such a thing?"

Fargo's estimation of her rose. Before he could respond, there was a commotion at the main stairs, and Captain Benjamin Bettles and the mate, a bear of a man by the name of Grear, appeared. Bettles was small and thin and had a close-cropped beard that failed to hide the fact he had no chin. His brown eyes nervously flitted from the two roustabouts to Amanda Stain to Fargo.

"I say, sir, what is the meaning of this? Am I to gather you have manhandled two of my crew?"

"Only after they manhandled one of your passengers," Fargo said with a nod at Amanda.

Finn had been on his knees, wheezing like a kicked goat, but now he struggled to his feet and growled, "That's a damned lie!"

Fargo's Colt leaped into his hand, and he swept it in an arc that caught Finn across the temple and felled him like a poled ox. In the same smooth motion, he returned it to his holster and hooked his thumbs in his gun belt.

Captain Bettles was momentarily speechless. Then he cleared his throat and nervously declared, "That was uncalled for. I must insist you turn over that firearm to me. I am confining you to your cabin for the remainder of your stay on board my vessel."

Grear started forward. He had a craggy face split by a jagged scar down the left side. Wedged under his wide leather belt was a bowie.

"Don't even think it," Fargo warned, dropping his right hand to the Colt.

Grear froze, and Captain Bettles puffed out his cheeks like an angry chipmunk. "See here! I am in command. A captain's word is law, and you will do as I say or I will give the signal, and you'll have every hand on board to deal with."

There was only so much Fargo would abide. He disliked Bettles. Not because the steamboat's skipper was weak-willed and let the crew get away with things most captains would not tolerate. Nor because Bettles was incompetent and had run the *Northern Lights* onto sand bars eleven times on their long trip up the Missouri River. No, he disliked Benjamin Bettles because the man was a pompous little jackass. "Go ahead and call your crew," he said, "if you don't mind losing six or seven. And if they don't mind losing their captain."

"You dare threaten *me*?"

Grear was fingering the hilt of his bowie. "Let me and the roosters deal with him, sir."

Rooster, as Fargo knew, was river slang for roustabout. He was about resigned to having to fight for his life when Amanda Stain stepped up and poked Bettles in his skinny chest.

"That will be quite enough, Captain. Mr. Fargo was only doing what he has been paid to do. Your men, on the other hand, reek of alcohol and were quite insulting. The issue isn't his behavior; it's theirs."

Bettles was too flustered to say anything.

"If you persist with these silly antics," Amanda said harshly, "I will inform my brother of how I was mistreated, and he will inform the owner." She paused masterfully. "This steamboat is owned by Mr. William Kitteredge of New Orleans, is it not?"

Captain Bettles deflated like a punctured water skin. "Please, Miss Stain, there is no need to bring the owner into this. I apologize for my crew, and I promise you this will never happen again." He glanced meaningfully at Grear.

Amanda smiled and said sweetly, "Thank you ever so much. I appreciate your sincerity." Then she extended an elbow to Fargo. "I believe I will take you up on your gracious offer. If you would be so kind as to escort me below, I would be ever so grateful."

Fargo waited until they were past the stairs and moving along the passenger compartments to say, "That was some act you put on."

Her green eyes were sparkling. "How else does one deal with idiots? The important thing is I spared you from more violence."

"I didn't know you cared." The warm feel of her arm and the tantalizing fragrance of her expensive perfume set Fargo to imagining how she would look without the dress.

"Don't flatter yourself," Amanda said. "I did it because we need you to get where we're going, and no other reason."

"If you say so." Fargo liked how her lovely face colored pink. "I'm ever so grateful," he mimicked her, and brushed his hand across her fingers.

Amanda said indignantly, "I should slap you. You're no better than those loutish roustabouts."

"But you won't."

"How can you be so sure?" Amanda retorted, and hefted her parasol as if she were thinking of striking him with it.

"You don't like violence, remember?" Fargo gazed past the railing at high bluffs hemming the river and a hawk that wheeled in the sky in search of prey.

"I never said I wouldn't defend my honor if I had to," Amanda said tartly.

"It's not your honor so much as your life you have to worry about," Fargo set her straight. "Dakota Territory isn't New Orleans. Once we're off this boat, we're in Sioux country. In case you haven't heard, they hate whites, and if they catch us, they'll separate you from that pretty hair of yours right before they slit your pretty throat."

"Are you trying to scare me?"

"I'm trying to get you to see that this loco quest your family is on can get all of you killed. Hostiles aren't your only worry. There are bears and buffalo and outlaws, fierce heat and scarce water."

"Goodness gracious," Amanda said lightheartedly. "Next you'll have me in dread of prairie dogs and grasshoppers."

Fargo should have known better. He had tried to talk her brother out of their harebrained notion when they approached him in St. Louis, where Thomas Stain had tracked him down. Thomas wanted to hire him for top dollar as a guide. Most men in Fargo's boots would gladly have agreed without a word of warning, but Fargo felt it only fair to give the Stains some idea of what they were in for. They shrugged it off. The whole family was that way. Too much confidence and not enough common sense.

"No comment?" Amanda bantered.

"If you want to get yourselves killed, be my guest," Fargo said testily. In his opinion some people had no business daring the rigors of the wilderness, and the Stain clan was at the top of the list.

"Evidently I have more confidence in your abilities than you do," Amanda said. "You're supposed to be the best there is at what you do. Scout, frontiersman, plainsman, whatever you care to call yourself, you have quite a reputation. My brother learned all about you."

As if on cue, a cabin door opened ahead and out stepped Thomas Stain. Like his sister, he was dressed in the best clothes his wealth could buy. His hat was tilted at a rakish angle, his suit impeccable. In his left hand was a polished cane with an ivory handle. "Sis! Mr. Fargo. I'm on my way to the boiler deck for some fresh air." He swiped at a speck of lint on his sleeve. "I can't stand to be cooped up for very long."

Fargo couldn't either. He preferred the vast prairie, the towering Rockies. Spending weeks inside a cramped compartment was enough to have him hankering after wide open spaces.

"Join me, won't you?" Stain requested, and headed aft without waiting for a reply.

"Your brother takes too much for granted," Fargo said.

"He's accustomed to having others do as he wants," Amanda responded. "He's a leader of men, not a follower."

"Even so, how can you let him drag you and your sisters off into the middle of nowhere?"

"First off, he's not dragging us; it's our mutual decision. Second, people travel across the prairie all the time. Wagon trains go from St. Joe to Oregon and freight trains from Kansas City to Santa Fe. It's a lot safer than you would have us believe."

Why was it, Fargo wondered, that some people always had an answer for everything? He had lived on the frontier nearly all his life. His roaming had taken him from the Mississippi River to the Pacific Ocean, from Canada to Mexico. He had experienced the blistering oven of the southwestern deserts, the bitter cold of snowcapped mountain peaks. He had lived with Indian tribes, tangled with others. Few men, white or red, had seen as much of the frontier as he had, yet here was Amanda Stain, who had never set foot west of New Orleans her whole life long, telling him that they had nothing to worry about.

The boiler deck was not as crowded except to starboard where Fargo saw a group of passengers he recognized. There was Charles Stain, older brother to Thomas and Amanda, and their sisters, Elizabeth and Emma. There was William Peel, a distant cousin, whose hair was as oily as his manner. There was Pompey, a black manservant, and Monique, the family maid, a petite, truly beautiful young woman. Finally, there was Maxton, who hovered in the background like a vulture waiting for a feast of carrion.

"It looks like everyone wanted fresh air," Fargo said.

Thomas twirled his cane. "Since we will be disembarking in a few days, I thought it wise to hold this meeting, as it were, to settle any last minute issues which might be raised."

"I have one," Fargo mentioned. "You still haven't told me where the hell you want to go." All Stain had revealed was that they wanted him to guide them north across the prairie from a certain point on the river. "Why all the secrecy?"

"I have my reasons," Thomas said. "But it won't do any harm to share a bit more information. You see, Mr. Fargo, we want you to find something for us."

When Stain did not go on, Fargo goaded him with, "What, exactly? A lost gold mine? A white buffalo? Wild horses?" At one time or another, he had been hired to find all three.

"No, no." Thomas Stain chuckled. "Nothing so silly, I assure you." He smiled broadly. "We're on a quest to find a ghost town."

No other series has this much historical action!

THE TRAILSMAN

Available wherever books are sold or at
www.penguin.com